James Martin

The Siege of Limerick

An Irish Military Drama

James Martin

The Siege of Limerick
An Irish Military Drama

ISBN/EAN: 9783744740708

Printed in Europe, USA, Canada, Australia, Japan

Cover: Foto ©Andreas Hilbeck / pixelio.de

More available books at **www.hansebooks.com**

St.

AN IRISH MILITARY DRAMA

IN FOUR ACTS.

SPECIALLY WRITTEN FOR THE

St. Ann's Young Men's Society,

By JAMES MARTIN,

(A MEMBER OF THE SOCIETY.)

MONTREAL.

St. Ann's Young Men's Hall, 157 Ottawa Street.

1897.

DRAMATIS PERSONÆ.

PATRICK SARSFIELD... Earl of Lucan... Irish General
ROGER O'GORMAN.....................An Irish Gentleman
DERMOT O'GORMAN................................His Son
HARRY NUGENT............... .... Dermot's Friend
COLONEL O'GRADY.........⎫
SERGEANT HAGAN...........⎬ Officers in the Irish Army
CORPORAL HOGAN.........⎭
THADY ....⎫
LARRY............................⎬ ...... Irish Gunners
MICKY CASSIDY ....A Lively Irish Boy
TIM BRANNIGAN....................His Faithful Friend
BARNEY O'REILLY...... ....A Blacksmith
DAN O'RAFFERTY....................... ....His Assistant
CONSIDINE ....An Irish Car-man
RORY MAGUIRE .... An Irish Sentinel
BEAUJACQUES........ ....A "Brave" Domestic
COLONEL BRECKENRIDGE..A Loyal Soldier of the King
SERGEANT BLAKELY........⎫
CORPORAL BINGLEY.........⎬ ......In the King's Army
SURGEON............................. ....

IRISH SOLDIERS, ENGLISH SOLDIERS, PEASANTS, ETC.

THE SIEGE OF LIMERICK.

ACT I.

SCENE —Room in Roger O'Gorman's House. TIM BRANNIGAN *discovered alone.*

TIM—(*Dusting furniture, etc*). Well, well, but queer times have come to Ireland! Not a one of us but's afraid to show his nose out of doors for fear of the sogers! (*Sits down*), Oh dear, oh dear, the life's tired out of me, an' I'm thinkin' I'll soon give up my position in the house of Roger O'Gorman. Once upon a time he was a fine man, an' what's better, a good Irishman, but oh! he's a changed man. When I was a youngster he was a good christian, but now he's a what-dy'e-call-it—a haythen, an' an infidel. I never see him goin'to chnrch for he's goin' to the divil. He never says his prayers, but he swears like a throoper. Sure only for young Masther Dermot I'd be gone long ago. Ah, but he's the fine man! There's an Irish boy for you! Time an' again has his father tried to change him, an' make an infidel or a haythen out of him, but it's no use. He sticks to the teachin's of his dead mother— the Lord be good to her—an' I'd be willin' to bet ten pounds that he always will.

(*Enter* MICKY CASSIDY *laughing immoderately.* TIM *starts to his feet*).

TIM—Micky, what's the matter with ye?

MICKY—(*Doubled up with laughter*). Oh dear, oh dear, oh dear, oh dear! Ach, ha, ha, ha!

TIM—Micky Cassidy, what's the matter, I say!

MICKY—Ach, ha, ha, ha, ha! he, he, he he!

TIM—Micky, is it the colic ye have?

MICKY—(*Shaking his head*). No Tim, it's the—Ach, ha, ha, ha!

TIM—Well, of all the born idiots I ever saw you're the worst! Can't ye stop yer gigglin' an' tell us what it's all about!

MICKY—Oh my, oh my, I never laughed so much in me life before, an' the new man is the cause of it all.

TIM—The new man! What new man!

MICKY—Sure dont ye know that the masther is goin' to get rid of us all, un' put others in our places?

TIM—To get rid of us! An' is that where the funny part comes in?

MICKY—It is, for one of the new fellows is down stairs. He's a fierce-lookin' Frenchman but the greatest coward ye ever saw in yer life, an' we've been frightenin' the divil out of him for the last half hour. Come down an' see him.

TIM—(*Moving to door*). Oh, if there's any fun goin' on I'm yer man.

(*Exeunt R. Enter ROGER O'GORMAN, L*).

O'G.—(*Looking around*). What! He has not come yet! Well, I will wait. I know he will attend my summons. (*Seats himself at a desk*). And when he does come, will I do as I have always done—or will I once and forever crush the spirit within him and force him to obey my will! We shall see. The battle between us has been long and stubborn. Hh has thwarted me; he has refused to become what I am—a supporter of the King, and worse than all he clings with a dogged tenacity to the religion I hate. Bah! He takes after his mother—a fanatic. But he must obey me, he *shall* bow to my dictates. (*Opens a drawer and takes out some papers and in doing so allows a locket to fall to the floor. He picks it up*). What! How came this here! The picture of my wife—my wife when she became my bride! How sadly her eyes look into mine!—Good heaven, the thing is bewitched! The eyes seem to move—to rivet themselves upon mine! There, there is the look I saw upon her dying face as her voice wailed in my ears "Spare my son"! (*Enter DERMOT who stands looking at his father, in surprise. O'G. throws the locket into the drawer*). Away, phantom of the past! The echo of your last words must ever ring in my ears but your prayer shall be unheeded. Your son is also mine, and I shall bend him to my will. The Irish people must find in him a tyrant, and above all he shall and will turn his back upon his God!

DERMOT—Never, father, never while life is left to me!

O'G.—What! Eavesdropping!

DERMOT—No. I came here obedient to your call, and I entered just in time to hear your terrible language. (*Throws himself wearily into a chair*). But I am accustomed to it now, for I seldom hear your voice without being compelled to listen to denunciations of the unfortunate Irish people, and alas! blasphemous utterances against that God whom you once served.

O'G.—God! God! Ever the same word from your lips. Speak not of God to me for I have renounced him! The only God I acknowledge is that inward voice which urges me to uproot and destroy every thing connected with religion. And now the time has come. To-morrow I join the army of the King. True, he claims not to war against religion, but he wars against the Irish, and in the ranks of his army I will slake my thirst for revenge!

DERMOT—(*Rising*), What! You, an Irishman, would aid the enemies of your own country! You, the son of an Irishman turn your sword against your struggling Irish brothers ! No, no, you are jesting—you could not do it !

O'G.—I can and I will. Sit down, I have something more to tell you. Some years ago you learned of my hatred for religion and for the Irish, but I never told you my reasons, and before taking the final step, I wish to make them known to you.

DERMOT—Pardon me, father. Before you utter a word of explanation let me tell you, that the brightest intellect, the most logical reasoner on the face of this broad earth has never found, and never will find a cause sufficient to justify a man in becoming a traitor to his country or to his God !

O'G.—Wait, have patience ; hear me, and then judge me.

DERMOT—Pardon me again, I know your object—'tis the same which, for the past ten years, has upheld you in your determination to change me from what I am. It was my beloved mother who implanted in my soul a love for the Eternal, She, alas ! is dead, but her spirit lives within me. On the other hand my heart has ever throbbed in sympathy with my oppressed fellow-countrymen, and if I were offered riches, honors or titles in return for my treason, I would spurn them and tell the tempter that in my ears ring the bells of freedom, and their glorious sound shall not cease until my heart is cold in death !

O'G.—Rash boy, perhaps that hour approaches !

DERMOT—Father I would welcome it if within that hour I were sure of your return to the Almighty, for then evil would have lost a champion in Roger O'Gorman, and sorrowing, bleeding Ireland have gained a defender.

O'G.—Idle words, idle hopes, and I will tell you why. Many years ago I had a friend—a bosom friend. He wronged me, I swore vengeance. I was then a Catholic In due time I went to confession. The priest ordered me to forgive my enemy. I refused. He denied me the Sacraments. This enraged me. He who had had wronged me was an Irishman—I now saw an enemy in every one of his race. The priest offended my pride—I swore vengeance against the Church, and to-morrow I shall begin my work !

DERMOT—Begin your work, did you say ? Alas ! the beginning is now far in the past. Ever since I was a child your unreasoning hatred of every thing Irish has been a painful problem to me. You have been so tyrannical in your dealings with the common people that you have earned the title of "Cruel." Father, let me warn you. As you know, the Irish people, goaded to fury, have risen against their oppressive rulers. The tide of war is spreading ; those whom you have treated so harshly, are taking up arms. Beware, beware of the vengeance of an outraged people !

O'G.—What ! Do you think that I, Roger O'Gorman, should run from a handful of half-clad rebels whose threats are not worth that ! (Cracks his fingers).

DERMOT—Yes, they are poorly clad, but their lack in that respect will not take the strength from their arms, the patriotism from their hearts, nor will it dampen the noble courage which inspires them to give their lives for Ireland and freedom !

O'G.—All nonsense, all nonsense ! The rabble will but give the King's troops a little practice. Mow them down ! Cut them to pieces ! Drive them from the face of the land ! But, enough of this : I called you here this morning for a double purpose, the first part of which I have already unfolded to you. And now for the second, which is this : to-morrow I leave here to join the army of the King, and—listen well,—you will accompany me.

DERMOT—For what purpose, father ?

O'G.—For the purpose of entering the ranks of the army under the banner of King William !

DERMOT—(Rising). What ! I join the ranks of the enemies of my country ! Father, this is a ghastly joke !

O'G.—You will find yourself face to face with a ghastly reality, if you refuse to obey me !

DERMOT—Then I refuse to obey ! Obedience to your parental authority has ever been to me a sacred thing, but this demand,—this interference with my rightful liberty,—this command to steep my hands in the blood of my gallant countrymen shall not be obeyed !

O'G.—Do you know the alternative ?-

DERMOT—I know that I will incur your anger ; that you will attempt to force me to obey, but although you may command my body, you cannot fetter my soul !

O'G.—No, perhaps I cannot break your stubborn will, but I can, and if you still refuse to obey me, I shall hand you over to the authorities to be shot as a rebel !

DERMOT—You would not do that !

O'G.—Ah, you grow pale ! You shrink at my threat ! You tremble with fear !

DERMOT—Yes, I tremble, but not with fear of dying for love of my country, but at the terrible thought that my father,—that Roger O'Gorman, should stoop to utter such a threat to his own son, and in such a cause !

O'G.—You still refuse !

DERMOT—Yes, and will never alter my decision. Listen to me for I too, have something to tell. A few days ago I performed an action which I know will lead me in the path of honor and duty—duty to my fellow-man,

O'G.—What do you mean !

DERMOT—That I have already taken a step similar to that which you contemplate taking to-morrow.

O'G.—What! Have you then been merely joking with me this morning! Have my years of patience and striving been crowned with success! You have entered the army!

DERMOT—Yes, I have enrolled myself in an army, but one vastly different from that of King William.

O'G.—There is none other. Explain yourself.

DERMOT—Yes, there is another and led by a man glorious in his achievements, grand in his aims; one whose mighty voice has awakened the echoes in our green isle, and before whose advance tyrants fall back, defeated and dismayed!

O'G.—And what army is this of which you seem to know so much! What do you call this valiant aggregation.

DERMOT—The army of Ireland!

O'G.—A rather high-sounding title for a mob of hungry peasants! And who commands this army!

DERMOT—One whose name is known and revered over all Ireland, loved by Erin's friends—feared by her foes.

O'G.—His name—his name!

DERMOT—Patrick Sarsfield!

O'G.—You are mistaken. Sarsfield has left Ireland, disgusted alike with the land and its people.

DERMOT—No; at the head of his troops he is driving his enemies before him, and under his flag, which is the green banner of Ireland, at least one O'Gorman shall be found!

O'G.—Then that one shall not be of my house! You have chosen to disobey and defy me, (moves to door) you have compelled me to act, and I shall act!

DERMOT—Father, stop and hear me. What will it avail you if your threat is carried out! My death would not affect the cause of my country, but in the future it would occasion you infinite remorse. Oh, my father, forget the past! Throw aside those terrible years of hatred of God and your country, Let the light from above enter your soul, let your own heart assert itself, and then The O'Gorman shall be true to his race!

O'G.—Stop! Your words are an insult to me. You have chosen your path and I will choose mine!

(Exit O'Gorman).

DERMOT—Stern and unyielding as ever! Non-success in his efforts to lead me away from every thing I hold dear has embittered him, until now he is capable of putting his threat into execution. But I shall not allow him to commit such a crime. I will save both myself and him.

(A knock at the door. Enter HARRY NUGENT).

DERMOT—Harry Nugent! Why, my dear fellow, what is the matter!

HARRY—Oh, great news, Dermot ! You know it was the intention to send us, that is you and me and the rest of the new regiment, to Galway, where, upon my word, we would'nt have a bit of fighting to do, but half an hour ago, our colonel came tearing in like a mad man with the glorious news that we're off to Limerick at seven o'clock to-night. Give me your hand !

(Shake hands).

DERMOT—To Limerick, you said ?

HARRY—Yes, and faith to look at the way you take it, one would imagine I had said Russia ! What is wrong, Dermot ?

DERMOT—I will tell you, for I don't think I ever kept a secret from you yet, for I trust you.

HARRY—(*Laying his hand on D's shoulder*). Thank you, my boy, and you may continue to do so.

DERMOT—I know it. But come and sit down. (*Take chairs*). Matters between my father and me have reached a climax. Things, as you know, have been going from bad to worse for some time and a few minutes ago I had an audience with my father. You are aware of his hostility to every thing Irish so I need'nt go into that. It is too painful a subject.

HARRY—I know it, my poor fellow and you have my sympathy. Go ahead.

DERMOT—He gave me a piece of intelligence that, alas ! I might have expected. He leaves here to-morrow to join the ranks of our enemies.

HARRY—Ha, ha ! It has gone so far as that ?

DERMOT—Yes, and worse still, he has commanded me to follow and do likewise.

HARRY—What ! Do you mean to say that he wants you to—Oh confound it ! However, you did'nt consent, of course ?

DERMOT—No, I not only refused, but told him that I had already enlisted in the Irish army.

HARRY—That's right. And what did he say to that ?

DERMOT—Oh, how can I tell you ? But if I stay here another hour the whole county will know it. He is half mad, I think, else he would not dream of handing over his own son to the executioner !

HARRY—My God, O'Gorman ! What do you mean ? Hand you over to the executioner ?

DERMOT—Yes ; frenzied at hearing what I had done he passionately vowed to declare me a rebel, and you know what that means.

HARRY—Don't I know it ! Yes, for only yesterday poor Tom O'Mahoney was dragged from his house at Cork and hanged like a dog ! Quick, let us go—but, man, surely your father would not do such a thing ?

DERMOT—Alas! I know him well. He is adamant once his mind becomes fixed upon anything, and his disappointment as regards myself has rendered him rash unto madness.

HARRY—Well then, we have not a moment to lose, for before night that infamous scoundrel, Colonel Brockenridge, the same that ordered the execution of poor O'Mahoney, will have arrived from Cork, and at all hazards we must get ahead of him. Our uniforms and accoutrements are in the old school-house, where at the present moment, the boys are getting ready for the march. Quick, let us be off.

DERMOT—Yes, your advice is good and I will take it, but before going I must see my father once again. Perhaps he will become softened towards me, and if not, still I may—anyway I must see him again before I leave, and whether I succeed or fail you may depend upon seeing me within an hour.

HARRY—All right; I'll depend upon you.

(*Exeunt R. door. Enter* O'GORMAN L.)

O'G.—(*Producing a note*). This will bring him to understand that I am not to be trifled with! (*Reads note*) "*This is to notify you that a rebel is at this moment within my house. Send at once and effect his arrest.*"

(*Rings bell*).

I will see him dead,—shot as a traitor, before I allow my enemies to gloat over the fact that I had reared a boy to fight for a cause I hate and for a people I despise!

(*Enter* TIM).

(*To* TIM). Take this to the Commandant at the barracks and be quick about it!

TIM—Is it to the Ould Major ye mean? The fellow that nearly broke his neck runnin' away from a handful of patriots the other day?

O'G.—None of your insolence, but do as you are told, and tell Cassidy to come here at once.

TIM—(*Aside*). May the divil take the ould haythen! Bad cess to him I'll not stay with him another day.

(*Exit, making a grimace as he goes out*).

O'G.—(*Seating himself*). Was there ever a man in such a position as that in which I now find myself? I a firm upholder of the King and parliament whilst my son clings to every thing that I have renounced, and despite my years of effort to win him over. But I must conquer him; his will shall be broken. Arrest and imprisonment will succeed where my words have failed, and if not—if he still hold out against my commands, if he persist in his determination to thwart me then he shall die!

(Enter CASSIDY).

(To CASSIDY). Cassidy, I am going to my room and on no account do I wish to be disturbed. Do you understand?

CASS.—I do, sir, I do

O'G—Mark me well—no one, I say no one, must be permitted to come to me!

(Moves to door).

CASS. —All right, sir.

(Exit O'G).

What's wrong with the old boy, I'd like to know? He looks as if he was about to swallow us all! Begorra I'm afraid there's trouble brewin' between Maather Dermot and his hard-hearted father, an' what'll come of it I don't know. There have been queer goin's on in this house for the last fortnight; soldiers,—men that should never be allowed to darken the door of an Irishman—that is if he's the right kind—have been hob-nobbin' with the maather, an' knowin' the man as I do, I fear there's somethin' wrong. Sure, on account of what we are, not a one of us would be kept in this house a minute, only he can't get any one else—except that omadhaun of a Frenchman down stairs, an' he— oh, begorra, he's a beauty !

(Enter DERMOT).

DERMOT—Cassidy, do you know where my father is ?

CASS.—He's in his room, Maather Dermot, but just this minute he told me that he does'nt want anyone to disturb him.

DERMOT—*(Moving to door).* I must see him and at once.

CASS.—Ah, for the love o' God, Maather Dermot, don't go near him, or he'll break every bone in my body !

DERMOT—Nonsense man, I must see him !

CASS.—Well then, wait a minute an' I'll go an' tell him.

DERMOT—Very good.

(Exit CASSIDY).

Can it be possible that he will not see me ? Has he ordered the servants to refuse me admittance to his presence ? Surely not, and yet it may be so. All love for me, his only son, cannot yet be dead within him, and he may fear that my pleading will move him in spite of himself.

(Throws himself into a chair).

Ah, the future looks dark and threatening My father, the descendant of the liberty-loving O'Gormans, has torn himself away from the traditions of the past, and, may God forgive him ! has given himself body and soul to our enemies But I will save him yet, yes, even if I give my life as a sacrifice !

(Re-enter CASSIDY).

DERMOT—Well ! He will see me !

CASS.—I—I don't know, but he gave me this for you.

(*Hands note*).

(*Aside*). Begorra, for ten pounds I would'nt tell the poor fellow what his ould curmudgeon of a father said !

(CASSIDY *busies himself about the room*).

DERMOT—He refuses to see me ! (*Reads note*). " *Do not attempt to come near me. It will be useless* " (*Drops note*). At last the chain which has bound our destinies to ether is broken ! To-morrow my father departs on his mission of vengeance upon those who never harmed him, and—oh God ! the thought is horrible. My own father to give me into the hands of those who thirst for the blood of every Irishman who is true to his country ! But no, they shall not find me ! I will live to save him who would destroy me. I will live to save my father from himself and from the devil that pursues him !

(*About to leave*).

CASS.—Masther Dermot, what is wrong !

DERMOT— Cassidy, you have always been a faithful fellow and I will tell you My father and I have quarreled and I am going away to-night. His intention is to discharge all his people with the exception of the butler and one or two others. I want you to stay here, for you may be of service to me in the future. Will you do this !

CASS.—Will I ! Well such a question ! Sure ye know that I'd go to the end of the earth for you !

DERMOT—That is settled then. Good-bye till we meet again. (*Aside*). My father will not listen to me now, but, he *shall* hear my last appeal !

(*Exit* DERMOT).

CASSIDY—Well, upon my word, but things are lookin' bad. Masther Dermot is goin' away, but it's his ould sinner of a father that's sendin' him off, bad manners to him ! How will I get even with him for packin' us all about our business ? I have it. ! I'll torment him through his new man—the Frenchman !

(*Enter* TIM).

TIM—Micky, me boy, it's all up with us !

CASS.—How do you mean, Tim !

TIM—That long-legged, thick-headed ould divil of a butler has just told me that we're all goin' to be discharged except bimself an' the new Frenchman.

CASS.—I know that already ; Masther Dermot told me, an' look here Tim, the masther's in an awful way. He told me to let no one go near him an' only this minute he refused to see his own son. Between you an' me I think he has driven Masther Dermot from the house.

TIM—You don't say so ! Faith I know there's some divilment goin' on, for he gave me a letter for the commander of the barracks, but what it's about I dont know. I did'nt want to show my face there so I sent Flannagan with it.

CASS.—Look here Tim, just before ye came in I was thinkin' how we'd get even with the ould boy for drivin' us away, an' it struck me that we could get at him through the new man.

TIM—Who is that ? The Frenchman ?

CASS.—The very same.

TIM—How would you go about it, Micky ?

CASS.—Well, ye know yourself that he's as timid as a mouse, an' I think that between the two of us we can raise a revolution in this very house. Whisht ! here he comes.

(*Enter* BEAUJACQUES *with flour sprinkled over his clothes*).

BEAU.—Ah, Monsieur Cassidy, I was look for you over all.

CASS.—Ye were lookin' for me overalls ? Begorra ye look as if ye needed a pair ! What has happened to you ?

TIM—Faith, Micky, he's the flower o'the flock.

BEAU.—I was walk on de—what you call—de—de—escaliers—de stair you know, and I hear one shout, terrible, terrible, and I fall down wit de flour I was carry.

CASS.—Ye heard a shout, did you ?

BEAU.—Oh, yes, like some one who was murder or someting.

CASS.—Tim, I'll bet ye anything it was the ghost of poor Mrs. Hoolahan who was murdhered by the Masther last week because she did'nt cook the dinner right.

(BEAUJACQUES *begins to tremble*).

TIM—I'm sure it was for I've heard her meself.

BEAU.—Murder ! You say murder !

CASS.—Yes, of course. Ye see the poor woman was a new hand, an' one day she burned the mate for dinner. The masther called her up stairs an' says he, " Mrs. Hoolahan, did you cook the dinner to-day ? " " Yes, sir," says she. " Well," says he, " you're the divil's own cook for the mate is all burned," au' with that he picks up a knife from the table, killed her on the spot, an' then sat down au' ate his dinner as cool as ye please.

TIM—Yes, indeed ; I saw him do it.

BEAU.—Mon Dieu, dis is terrible ! And de law she not hang him for dat ?

TIM—Not at all ! Sure a little thing like that is not minded at all, here. Faith an' Mrs. Hoolahan is not the first he killed, for he has murdhered eighteen of his servants altogether since I have been here.

BEAU.—(*To* CASSIDY) Is dat so ?

CASS.—Oh, thrue as Gospel ! When the masther tells ye to do a thing, an' if ye dont do it right, he'll just whip a knife out of his pocket an' kill ye before ye can say Jack Robinson.

BEAU.—Ma foi, dis is frightful ! I will go away from dis house, and never come once more.

TIM.—Oh, that wouldn't help ye, for it's the same all over Ireland. Sure if ye're not always shoutin' " God save the King" ye're likely to be murdered at any minute in the day or night.

BEAU.—Gracious goodness ! And when you say "God save de King" dey not kill you !

TIM.—Oh, divil the kill, for then they think ye're one of themselves

CASS.—Yes, an' there's another way of appeasin' them, an' that is to shout " Hurrah for King Bi ly" as loud as ye can.

BEAU Hurrah for King Beely !

CASS —Yes ; that'll stop them right off.

BEAU.—And you say dat Monsieur O'Gorman kill seventeen or eighteen peoples !

CASS.—As dead as door nails, an' put their bodies into the cellar. That's how it is that ye hear groans an' strange noises wherever ye go through the house.

TIM.—Whist, Micky, I think the masther's comin'. Let us hide.

(TIM and CASSIDY hide under pieces of furniture, leaving BEAU-JACQUES in the middle of the floor). Enter O'GORMAN.

O'G.—(Looking at BEAUJACQUES.)
What is the matter with you ?

BEAU.—I fall down stairs and spill some flour on me.

O'G.—You had better go and remove it. But wait—go up stairs and bring me a box you will find in a small room at the end of the corridor. Be quick now.

(Exit BEAUJACQUES). O'G. sits at a desk.)

TIM.—(From his hiding-place.) Micky, let us have some fun when Mist'er Beoujack comes back.

CASS.—What'll we do ?

TIM.—Oh, we can begin by lettin' a groan or two out of us. (A loud noise as of a large box falling down stairs. O'G. rises.)

O'G.—What can that b ? (Enter BEAUJACQUES pulling a large packing case after him.)

BEAU.—Eh, by gosh, dis is a heavy box !

O'G —What are you doing there ?

BEAU.—Dis is de box I find on de leetle room, monsieur.

O'G.—I don't want that thing. Take it out of here

BEAU.—All right, monsieur. (He is about to remove the box when a groan from TIM disturbs his balance and he falls over the box.)

O'G.—What is the matter with you !

BEAU.—(Rising and trembling.) Ah ! You not hear it !

O'G.—Hear what !

BEAU.—One large groan.

O'G.—A large groan! What are you talking about!

BEAU.—Ah, mon Dieu, it is terrible!

O'G.—I think you are out of your mind. Hurry up and take back that box to where you found it. (*Another groan from* TIM, *followed by one from* CASSIDY, *which elicit a yell from* BEAUJACQUES.)

O'G.—Why in thunder do you raise such a disturbance in my house! What do you mean, sir!

BEAU.—Ah, I will go away. I cannot stay on dis house. You not hear two groans!—terrible groans!

O'G.—Confound it, man, I heard nothing but the noise made by yourself!

BEAU.—Ah, no, I not make dat groans. It was Madame Hoolahan.

O'G.—Madame Hoolahan! What are you talking about!

BEAU.—Ah, yes, poor Madame Hoolahan.

O'G.—I think you are mad. Who is this Madame Hoolahan!

BEAU.—Dat was de cook.

O'G.—What cook!

BEAU.—Dat was your cook.

O'G.—Madame Hoolahan! My cook! You are raving!

BEAU.—No, no; dat was de cook dat burned de meat.

O'G.—(*Aside*). I think I have a lunatic on my hands. (*Aloud*) Where is this cook you are talking about!

BEAU.—She is on de cellar.

O'G.—In the cellar! What is she doing there!

BEAU.—She is dead.

O'G.—Dead! A woman dead in my cellar! (*Takes a step or two forward.*)

BEAU.—(*Trembling.*) Ah, yes, but I not tell nobody.

O'G.—You will not tell what!

BEAU.—Dat it was you what kill her.

O'G.—Look here, my fine fellow, if I see you in this state again I shall discharge you. You are drunk.

BEAU.—No, no, no! It is true you kill de cook, but I say notting, for dat is no harm on dis country; dey all kill de peoples.

O'G.—Well, upon my word you are enough to provoke a man to murder. Leave the room at once! (*Advances threateningly.*)

BEAU.—(*Falling on his knees.*) No, no, do not murder me! Do not kill me! (*Very loud.*] God save de King! God save de King!

O'G.—What is the matter with you!

BEAU.—God save de King! (*Louder*). God save de King!

O'G.—Stop your hideous yelling, or I shall—

BEAU—God save de King!

(*Exit O'G. with his hands over his ears.*)

— 15

BEAU.—(*Rising.*) Ah, dat was a narrow escape! I was nearly kill only for dat God save de King. I must leave dis place very quick or I will be a dead mans——

(*Several groans from* TIM *and* CASSIDY, BEAUJACQUES *stands trembling and finally rushes out* R. CASSIDY *and* TIM *emerge from their hiding places.*)

TIM.—Ah, ha, ha, ha, Micky me boy, hold me sides or I'll burst, upon me word I will.

CASS.—Tim,—Ha, ha, ha, will ye tell me how long the new man'll stay here! Haw, haw, haw.

TIM.—Begorra, Micky, I think he'll stay till he gets out of the house, ha, ha, ha.

CASS.—Hush—somebody's comin'. Perhaps it's the masther, an' if it is we'd better get out.

(*Exeunt* L. *Re-enter* BEAUJACQUES, *cautiously.*)

BEAU.—Parbleu, I cannot get down on dis side ; dere is no stairs. What can I do?

(*A knock at* L. *door.* BEAUJACQUES *trembles, but remains where he is. The knock is repeated. Enter* COLONEL BRECKENRIDGE.)

COL.—(*Looking at* BEAUJACQUES.) In the name of Mars, what have we here?

BEAU.—Eh? What is dat?

COL.—Is Mr. O'Gorman in?

BEAU.—No—dat is—yes—

COL.—Well, which is it—yes or no?

BEAU.—Let me go away ; I want to leave dis house!

COL.—(*Barring the way.*) Wait a minute : I should say that you are a house-breaker! Where is Mr. O'Gorman?

BEAU.—I know not, and I did not break any houses, but if I not go away I will broke my neck.

COL.—Well, if not a thief, what are you? Mr O'Gorman's servant?

BEAU.—No, no, I am notting at all. I came here for work every day, but I not stay.

COL.—However, since you are here will you inform Mr. O'Gorman that Colonel Breckenridge wishes to see him?

BEAU.—Monsieur O'Gorman! Ah, no, I not go near Monsieur O'Gorman!

COL.—You will not go near him! Why, has he a fever and you are afraid of infection?

BEAU.—No, I not afraid of confection, but I not like to be murder!

COL.—(*Aside.*) This is either a knave or a fool ; however, I shall humor him. (*Aloud.*) Oh, I don't think Mr. O'Gorman or any one else would kill a man of your calibre.

BEAU.—Calibre! Calibre! I not know what is calibre, but he kill de cook.

COL.—He, what!

BEAU.—He murder de cook for burn too much de meat!

COL.—(*Laughing and seating himself.*) Well, well, you are a droll fellow. However, you should not be afraid of Mr. O'Gorman even if he did kill a cook or two.

BEAU.—Oh, he did kill more dan dat. He murder seventeen or eighteen peoples!

COL.—Dear, oh dear! I never thought O'Gorman was such a bloodthirsty man! Where did you get all this information?

BEAU.—(*Puzzled*). I have no information. I did not say dat.

COL.—I mean from whom did you get this rubbish?

BEAU.—(*Looking at his clothes*) Ah, dat's not rubbish; dat's flour. I fall down stairs and dat spill over me.

COL.—(*Aside*). This is a regular simpleton. (*Aloud*). Look here, my dear fellow, run and tell Mr. O'Gorman that I am here. I shall not allow him to hurt you, I assure you.

BEAU.—All right, I will go, but if he run after me to kill me, you will will say "Hurrah for King Billy," ah!

COL.—What is that you say?

BEAU.—I say if he want to kill me you will say "Hurrah for King Billy!"

COL.—(*Rising*). How dare you speak so disrespectfully of the King!

(TIM *and* CASSIDY *appear at I door*).

BEAU.—I not say any harm!

COL.—No harm! Do you consider it proper to apply the name of "Billy" to the King of England? Apologize! Apologize, sir! (*Lays hand on sword*).

BEAU.—(*Falling on his knees*). Ah, forgive me! God save de King! Hurrah for King Billy!

COL.—You dare to repeat the insult!

BEAU.—God save de King! God save de King! Hurrah for King Billy!

COL.—(*About to draw sword*). Another word and I shall—(*aside*) but pshaw! What am I doing? This is only a poor idiot who does not know what he is saying. (*Aloud*) Rise; I will not harm you.

BEAU.—(*Rising*). Ah, le bon Dieu! Dat is twice dese words save my life! Ma foi, but Monsieur Brannigan and Monsieur Cassidy are very clever peoples!

COL.—Listen to me my dear fellow: I would advise you to drop the name of Billy when speaking of the King. "Hurrah for King Billy" suits the Irish very well; but "God save the King" better agrees with the ear of a soldier. Get along now and tell Mr. O'Gorman I wish to see him.

BEAU.—Ah, yes, I will go. (*Moves to door*). Now I understand.

"Hurrah for King Billy" is for de Irish, and "God save de King" is for de soldiers. Ah, yes.

(He is about to go out when CASSIDY *and* TIM *give utterance to a moan and shut the door.)*

Oh, le bon ciel! Dare it is again! You not hear it!

COL.—I heard something like a moan. *(Looking around).* What is it?

BEAU.—Ah, dont speak loud! Dat is Madame Hoolahan!

COL.—Where is she? Is she ill?

BEAU.—Ah no, she is dead!

COL.—Dead! Why, man, if she were dead she would be unable to utter a sound!

(Enter O'GORMAN R. *door.)*

BEAU.—Yes, but she was murder! She was kill by Monsieur O'Gorman!

O'G.—What is that fellow saying, Colonel?

COL.—Upon my word he has said that you have murdered a Madame Hoolahan!

O'G.—*(To* BEAU.) How dare you say such things, you scoundrel!

BEAU.—Ah, Monsieur O'Gorman, forgive me! Hurrah for King Billy!

COL.—*(To* BEAU.) Did I not tell you not to speak those words, you rascal!

BEAU.—*(To the* COLONEL.) God save de King! God save de King!

O'G.—Stop your bawling and get out of this room!

BEAU.—*(To* O'GORMAN.) Hurrah for King Billy! Hurrah for King Billy!

COL.—You will say that again?

BEAU.—*(To the* COLONEL.) God save de King! God save de King!

O'G.—You will not leave the room? Then I shall comp'l you. *(He seizes* BEAU, *and lifting him to his feet, forcibly ejects him.)*

BEAU.—*(As he goes out.)* God save de King! Hurrah for King Billy! God save de King!

(Exit BEAU.)

COL.—*(As* O'G. *returns)* Tell me, O'Gorman, have you many such as he in your service?

O'G.—No, thank the fates, he is the only one. I engaged him this morning. The fellow is thoroughly mad, and some way or other has got it into his head that I have been guilty of a couple of murders. But, enough of him. What is the news from Cork?

COL.—Upon my word, O'Gorman, the very worst possible! Where is your son?

O'G.—My son! What of him?

COL.—Now, O'Gorman, but for my personal knowledge of both yourself and your feelings for the Irish, the news I have heard would compel me to look upon you as a traitor to the King!

O'G.—Colonel Breckenridge, you forget yourself!

COL.—Nonsense, man—let me explain. When in the City of Cork the other day, one of our secret agents informed me that Dermot, son of Roger O'Gorman, had raised a company of Irishmen, which company, with others, amounting in all to a full regiment, is to advance to the occupation of Limerick. I can see by your face that you are astonished.

O'G.—Astonished! I am bewildered!

COL.—I am not the least surprised that he should have done this but that he could accomplish it without your knowlenge is something I cannot understand. However, the harm is done, and we shall have to put up with it.

O'G.—Then I tell you that we shall not! Colonel, this morning, I had a talk with him. I urged him to link himself with me in the service of the King, but he refused, openly defied me, and boasted of the fact that he had already joined what he calls the army of Ireland.

COL.—And he has done so with a vengeance for he is already a captain under the seal and authority of Patrick Sarsfield, Earl of Lucan.

O'G.—Then he shall meet his doom—the doom of a rebel! In the hope of coercing him to obedience, I decided to cause his arrest, feeling that such a course would subdue him, and now nothing shall save him!

(Rings bell).

COL.—What are you about to do?
O'G.—To summon him to our presence.

(Enter CASSIDY).

Cassidy, tell my son that I wish to see him.
CASS.—Yes, sir. *(Aside.)* Begorra, the boy is out of harm's way an' the divil himself couldn't catch him.

Exit CASSIDY.

O'G.—I expect a squad to arrive at any moment, for I have sent an urgent message to the barracks.

COL.—O'Gorman, remember that the boy is your son.

O'G.—I can remember nothing—nothing but the fact that he has cast aside my authority, that he has leagued himself with the people I detest, the people I have sworn to destroy, and he shall be the first to fall!

COL.—Perhaps you are right. Of course such a proceeding on your part will set matters right at headquarters, where, to say the least, you are looked upon with suspicion.

(Re-enter CASSIDY.)

CASS.—*(To O'GORMAN.)* Masther Dermot is out, sir. He went away on horse-back some time ago.

O'G.—What ! He is gone ! Why did I not foresee this ! (*To* CASSIDY.) You may go.

(*Exit* CASSIDY.)

COL.—How will you proceed under the circumstances ! '

O'G.—I shall await the arrival of the soldiers, and then, if Dermot O'Gorman be upon this earth, he shall be found !

COL.—Hark ! What is that ! (*The tune " Garryowen" is heard as if at some distance, and gradually it becomes fainter and finally ceases. At the first sound of the music,* the COLONEL *and* O'GORMAN *step to the window, and* CASSIDY *appears at the door.*

COL.—What does this mean ! A body of troops wearing a green uniform !

CASS.—(*Aside.*) Faith it means that you an' the like of you will soon have your work cut out for you !

' COL.—They march like well-drilled troops !

. CASS.—(*Aside*). Why would'nt they ! Sure they are Irishmen.

COL.—Look ! look ! See them wheel !

CASS.—(*Aside*). Begorra they'll make you wheel by an' by.

COL.—They move in an easterly direction. O'Gorman, these are the fellows who are off to Limerick !

CASS.—(*Aside*). Faith yer right, an' God help the King's throops when they get there.

(*Exit* CASSIDY).

COL.—(*Wheeling*). But they shall never reach their destination ! O'Gorman, I must leave at once. I shall order an immediate pursuit—the devil ! What am I thinking of ! My regiment will not arrive for a couple of hours, for I rode ahead in my anxiety to see you, and there is but a handful of men in the barracks ! What shall I do !

(*A loud knock at the door. Enter* SERGEANT BLAKELY).

SERG.—(*Saluting*). Mr. O'Gorman, I await your orders.

O'G.—Ha, the sergeant from the barracks ! Sergeant the bird has flown ! Did you see a body of Irish troops on your way hither !

SERG.—I did, sir, but kept out of their way for I have only two men with me.

O'G.—(*To the* COLONEL). What can we do ! He will soon be out of our power. No doubt he is with those fellows, and is now on his way to Limerick.

COL.—(*To* SERGEANT). Sergeant, how many men are at the barracks !

SERG.—One hundred and twenty, sir.

COL.—Curse it ! And those fellows are fully a thousand strong. Hist ! What is that !

(*A commotion outside*).

SOLDIER'S VOICE—Halt, rebel !

DERMOT—(*Who is in uniform, outside*). Get out of my way !

(*More noise, and enter* DERMOT, *hurriedly. At first he sees only* O'GORMAN).

,DERMOT—Father, I have come to make a last appeal ——

(*Sees the* COLONEL *and* SERGEANT *and stops short*).

O'G.—(*To* DERMOT). You have arrived just in time ! Sergeant, there is the rebel !

(*Enter* TWO SOLDIERS).

SERG.—(*To* DERMOT). I arrest you in the name of the King ! (*To Soldiers*). Men, seize him !

(*A* SOLDIER *stands on either side of* DERMOT).

DERMOT—Father, I fear not death even if it were before me, but my heart bleeds when I see you in league with the enemies of our country, you who should be one of the first to draw your sword in her defence !

O'G—Away with him !

DERMOT—Father, hear me ——

(SOLDIERS *force him to* R).

O'G.—Not a word ! You have chosen to defy me, to laugh at my authority, and now you understand that I can force obedience to my commands ! But I shall give you a last chance to save yourself. Abjure the cause you have espoused, swear allegiance to the King of England, and you shall be pardoned !

DERMOT.—And be false to myself—false to honor and to manhood ! Swear allegiance to a King who persecutes us, and whose hands are red with the blood of my countrymen ! Never !

O'G.—Hesitate ! Death is before you ! Tear off those green rags——

DERMOT—Those green rags, as you term them are the badges of freedom, for beneath every green coat beats the heart of a man and a patriot, each one of whom is ready and willing to die in defence of the green flag that waves above him !

(*A few bars of the "Wearing of the green" which at first sound faint, but gat'er strength as the players appear to come nearer*).

COL.—(*At the window*). What is this ! Irish soldiers approaching !

O'G.—(*To the* TWO SOLDIERS). Quick ! This way !

(*About to move to* L. *door*).

DERMOT—Father, desist in your endeavors, they are useless——

O'G.—(*To* SOLDIERS.) Did you not hear me ! Drag him along ! (*A loud cheer is heard outside*)

A VOICE—Now boys, three cheers for Captain Harry Nugent. (*Renewed cheering*. SOLDIERS *endeavor to force* DERMOT *to* L. *Enter* HARRY NUGENT *in uniform*.

HARRY—(*Surprised at what he sees.*) O'Gorman a prisoner !
(*Draws his sword.*) Unhand him you scoundrels ! (SOLDIERS *release*
DERMOT. *The* COLONEL *draws his sword.*)

COL.—Rebel, surrender, in the King's name !

DERMOT—(*Stepping between the* COLONEL *and* NUGENT.) Nugent,
stand back ! It is I who must face this man !

HARRY—Faith you'll not ! Ho, there men.

(*Enter.* FOUR IRISH SOLDIERS,)

Cover these fellows, my lads ! Colonel Breckenridge, one movement
and I shall give the order to fire !

(*Enter* TIM *and* CASSIDY.]

CASS.—That's right, me boys ! More power to yer elbows !

TIM,—(*Looking towards the door.*) Boys, three cheers for Masther
Dermot and Captain Nugent ! Hip, hip, hip, hurrah ! (DERMOT
stands as though making a mute appeal to O'GORMAN.)

CURTAIN.

ACT II.

SCENE—A FORGE IN THE FOREST.. *A portable forge with necessary
tools, together with several pikes or spears.* BARNEY *and*
DAN *discovered, the former working the bellows while he
sings :*

BAR.—(*After the Song*). Dan, my boy, when I once get singin', I
dont know when to leave off, (*takes a spear-head out of the fire*), an' if
I had'nt taken this out of the fire, why, there'd be none of it left. Take
up your hammer there now an' give it a good poundin'. (*He places
his hammer in position, and (strikes several blows with a heavy
hammer*). There, that's it. (*Examines the spear*). Ah, is'nt that a
beauty ! Look at the color of it ! An' look at the shape of it ! An'
look at 'he point of it ! An' feel the weight of it ! Faith an' the boy
that carries it'll have no trouble with the enemy, for the man that could
stand forninst that, an' it pointed agin him has'nt been born yet, an'
never will be. Hand me that shaft Dan me honey, an' I'll soon show
you a pike fit for a lord.

DAN.—An' here's a shaft fit for the spear. I bought them meself this
mornin', an' they're all alike only one's setter than the other.

BAR.—Ah, that's what I call a handle for a pike !

(*Begins to fit the head to the shaft.*) Give me a good stout shaft, an'
I'll take care to turn out a pike that wo'nt go back on a man in a pinch.

(Lays the iron part on the anvil.) Just give it one sharp blow now. That's it. Hold on, I think it'll take another. That'll do. Now there you are me purty darlin', *(to the pike)* an' m·y ye do yer share in spoilin' the appetites of Ireland's-enemies. Dan, me boy, that's uncommon good wood. Where did ye get it !

DAN.—Down at Tom McGregor's, an' he keeps nothin' but the best.

BAR.—Faith I believe ye, for he's a mighty dacent fellow, an' although he's not an Irishman, still, Ireland has a good friend in that same Tom McGregor.

DAN.—Au' why should'nt he be, for he's a Scotchman, an' did'nt the Scotch, under the brave Dundee, batther the divil out of the same kind of fellows that's our enemies to-day ?

BAR.—Yer right, Dan, an' I wish a few thousan·' of his countrymen'd come over here au' give us a hand. But perhaps it's as well as it is, for I thiuk every country should fight its own battles.

DAN.—Well then I know at least one country that would'nt be of mitch account if it had to fight its own battles

BAR.—That's true for ye Dan, an' I know what ye mean. We Irishmen are so good-natured that all that same country has to do is to slap us on the back, palaver us a little, an' up we jump, give him our hand, fight for him like tigers, instead of catchin' him by the collar an kickin' him out of the house. Well, I don't think I'll do any more work to-day, for I've been at it since four o'clock this mornin' !

(Enter CASSIDY, TIM and a FEW PEASANTS).

CASS.—How are ye, how are ye, Barney ! All alive an' kickin' I hope !

BAR.—Is it Micky Cassidy ! And Tim Brannigan an' the rest of the boys ! Where did ye come from ?

CASS.—Ah, we were just havin' a look around an' we stumbled across ye. An' is it here ye've moved yer shop !

BAR.—Aye, faith, for the soldiers interfered with us too much in the town, an' it's out here we've come so as to be beyond their reach. Ye see, making pikes, at the present time, is a dangerous trade.

CASS.—Indeed an' it is, but sure that gives a relish to the work.

TIM.—Ah, Barney, have ye heard the news from Cork ?

BAR.—No, Tim, but I hope it's good ?

TIM.—Good ! Begorra it's the best I've heard for a long time. Ould Breckenridge has been defeated and driven out of the city, an' in the whole place there's not a single King's soldier to be found !

BAR.—Bully for you, good old rebel Cork !

CASS.—Yes, an' I have more news for you. You know young Dermot O'Gorman that joined the Irish army about two weeks ago !

BAR.—Do I know him ! Of course I do, an' a better lad never wore shoe-leather !

CASS.—Well, he was on the march to Limerick with the rest of his regiment, when they met with a large body of the enemy. There was a murdherin' big fight, an' our boys were beginnin' to give way, an' to make matters worse, the Irk': Colonel was struck by a ball an' killed. That seemed to take the heart out of our fellows, but there was somebody willin' an' able to take the Colonel's place. Now, I have this from an eye-witness. As I was sayin', the Irish began to give way, when out jumped Captain Dermot O'Gorman an' says he at the top of his voice. "Irishmen, are ye goin' to fall back before even twice yer number?" an' grabbin' hold of a flag, he pointed to it with his sword an' shouted, "Whoever deserts this flag is no longer an Irishman!" Begorra the boys stopped retreatin' an' looked at him. He saw he had them, so says he again, ' Men of Ireland, this is your first battle an' it must be won ; follow me an' it shall be won!" Faith, that settled it, an' in half an hour it was won.

BAR—More power to his elbow ! Yes, he's a fine young follow, an' it's a great pity his father isn't like him . Did ye hear anything of old O'Gorman ?

CASS.—Yes, may the divil fly away with him ! The auld haythanish Turk has gone off with Colonel Breckenridge, an' they've made a major out of him for his treachery. Barney ye've quite a stock of pikes here I see.

(Examines one.)

Begorra, but isn't that a fine instrument ! Boys, look at that ! Did ye ever see anything like it ?

TIM.—Oh, Micky, that reminds me—d'ye remember the song ye used to sing down at Terry's when all the boys'd join in the chorus ! Let us have it man. It's the very thing for the present time.

ALL—Yes, Micky, out with out !

CASS.—Well, I'll try, if you boys'll give me a hand with it ?

ALL—We will, Micky, we will. *He sings. After the song, enter* SERGEANT BLAKELY *wearing a long coat which covers his uniform. He enters whistling ' St. Patrick's Day "*

CASS.—Who have we here, Barney ?

BAR.—The divil a know I know.

BLAKELY—(*With a brogue.*) The top of the mornin' to ye, boys.

BAR.—The same to you. A fine day, isn't it ?

BLAKELY—It is a splendid day. (*Looks around.*) Ah, me boys, I see that ye're gettin' ready for the enemy. What a fine lot of pikes ye have !

CASS.—(*Aside, to* TIM) Tim, I don't think that fellow is what he pretends to be.

BAR.—(*To* BLAKELY.) Yes, we're kept pretty busy.

BLAKELY.—What's the news from Limerick, d'ye know ?

BAR.—Oh, faith the boys are doin' fine .

BLAKELY—(*Aside.*) I have dropped into a rebel nest ! (*Aloud.*) Ah, sure the King's troops have no chance at all with our boys !

BAR.—Thrue for you, thrue for you.

CASS.—(*Aside, to* TIM.) Tim, my boy, I'm goin' to make an investigation. (*To* BAR.) Barney, when our friend here was comin' along a moment ago, he was whistlin' a tune that made me feel like havin' a dance. (*To* BLAKELY.) Misther—misther—

BLAKELY—Larry Power, at yer service.

CASS.—Well, Misther Power, a man that can whistle as yo, did, can dance an Irish jig, an' I'm goin' to challenge ye now to see who can keep up the longest. (*Aside*.) If he can't dance an Irish jig me suspicions are right.

BLAKELY.—Upon me word ye must excuse me, for I'm not much of a dancer.

CASS.—Nonsense, man, of course ye can dance. But where'll we get the music ?

TIM.—Faith an' that's easily settled, for Rory Maguire here always carries his flute with him. Have ye yer flute, Rory ?

RORY.—(A Peasant.) I have, I have.

TIM.—That's right. Now up with an Irish jig for these two boys, an' we'll see which is the best at it.

BLAKELY—Really, me friend, I'd rather ye'd thry with some of these lads, for I have'nt danced these five years, an' besides I'm a bit stiff with the rheumatism.

CASS.—Arrah, man, sure the music'll take all that out of ye. Strike up there, Rory, me boy.

(RORY plays a jig *and the two begin to dance, but* BLAKELY's *dancing shows that he knows nothing about it, and in passing him* CASSIDY *trips him up*)

CASS.—(*Assisting* BLAKELY *to his feet*.) I beg yer pardon. Sure I'm as clumsy as the divil.

(*Seizes* BLAKELY *by the collar and throws his coat open, displaying the uniform beneath*.)

Boys, look at this ! I knew I was right ! Ah, ha, Sergeant Blakely, ye thought ye'd steal a march on us, eh !

ALL.—A spy ! A spy !

CASS —What'll we do with him ?

ALL.—Hang him up ! He deserves it !

CASS.—No, no, boys, we'll not do that Our enemies 'd hang one of us if they caught us in the same way ; but, lads, let no murder stain the hands of Irishmen !

A PEASANT.—An' are ye goin' to let go a fellow that'll spy upon us, an' who'd bring us to our death if he could ?

CASS.—No ; we'll take good care that he does'nt escape, but we won't slay him in cold blood. If there's one among ye boys who wants the life of this man, let him step forward !

(*No one stirs*).

an investi-
n' along a
e havin' a

did, can
who can
ig me sus-

not much

'll we get

here always

two boys,

th some of
es I'm a bit

ye. Strike

's *dancing*
im CASSIDY

rdon. Sur?

, *displaying*

aut Blakely,

hang one of
murder stain

spy upon us,

ape, but we
s who wants

BAR.—You are right Cassidy. We'll commit no murder.

ALL.—Yes, Cassidy's right.

CASS —I knew I was talkin' to Irishmen ! (*To* BLAKELY). Sergeant Blakely, ye've committed a foul offence against us, but we'll spare yer life an' make no boast of it, either. We'd kill our enemies in fair fight in defence of our home and country, but we'll not murder an unarmed man, for that'd be a crime that'd call to Heaven for vengeance !

BAR.—Micky, give me yer hand, for in a few words ye've told what a *rale* Irishman is.

CASS —This man is our enemy, nevertheless, both by his trainiu' as well as by his natural inclination, an' it's only the part of a wise man to guard against such ; so I say that the best thing we can do is to hand him over as a prisoner of war.

TIM.—But how will we do that Micky ? Sure the nearest town that's occupied by the Irish troops is five miles off !

BAR.—I have it ! There's a little cabin up here where I store me tools, an' we can leave him there for a while, for in a very short time I expect some of the boys to come here for a load of pikes, an' they can bring him away with them.

(*An* ENGLISH SOLDIER *is now seen at L. hiding behind a tree*).

CASS.—The very thing. Where is the cabin, Barney ?

BAR.—Dan here'll go up an' show ye the place.

CASS.—All right ; come along Sergeant, for we'll have to put ye where ye can't hurt us.

(*All go out R. except* BARNEY *and* TIM. *The* ENGLISH SOLDIER *moves stealthily across to R. and disappears*).

BAR —Faith, Tim, it was a good thing for us that Micky saw through that fellow's game, for no doubt if he got away safe, ourselves an' a big stock of pikes that I have up beyond there would have been captured, for ye may be sure he'd come back with more behind him.

TIM —Oh, ye can trust Micky to circumvent those fellows every time. Begorra I think he could see a red coat through a stone wall ! (*Music : an Irish quick step*.) What is this ? The military ? *Look* L). Yes, but they're our own boys, an' I'm blind if Sergeant O'Hagan isn't one of them !

(*Enter* L O'HAGAN *and a few* IRISH SOLDIERS).

TIM.—How are ye, O'Hagan, me man ? Bless me if ye have'nt grown a foot or two since ye went to Limerick ! (*To the others.*) How are ye boys, how are ye all ?

BAR.—O'Hagan, by the powers ! Faith me boy I'd hardly know ye. An' what brings ye down this way ? Sure it's up in Limerick I thought ye were !

O'HAGAN.—And so we were for several days, but the Colonel sent

Dermot O'Gorman and a few others of the company on a special mission, and we're off again to Limerick in the morning.

BAR.—An' is O'Gorman with ye? Where is he?

O'HAGAN.—He's not with us at the moment, but he's coming up this way from the town below. I'm sorry, Barney, that we can't stay with you for awhile, but we're in a hurry and must be off. Good bye, and you too, Tim. Don't let the colleens forget us while we're away.

TIM.—Faith there's no danger of them forgettin' ye, O'Hagan. Good bye an' good luck to ye.

Exeunt SOLDIERS R.

BAR.—Tim, when I see the boys in green it's the most I can do to keep meself quiet an' not run off with them. But then I have me work to do here, an' work that must be done, too.

TIM.—Yes, Barney, there's a good reason why you should stay behind, but there's none for me, an' bad luck to me if I don't go off with Captain O'Gorman when he comes up. O'Hagan said he'd pass this way, an' when he does, Barney, ye can say good bye to Tim Brannigan.

Re-enter R. CASSIDY *and the peasants.*

BAR.—Well, Micky, is the bird safe in the cage?

CASS.—He is, indeed, an' so that he'd have no chance of escape we tied him up a bit.

BAR.—An' ye did right, Micky. D'ye know what Tim here is talking of doin'?

CASS.—No; what is it?

BAR.—He says he's goin' off to Limerick with Captain Dermot O'Gorman.

CASS.—With Captain O'Gorman! Sure he's not here?

BAR.—No, but he's comin' up this way.

CASS.—Well, then, if Tim goes so will I.

FIRST PEASANT—And I too.

SECOND PEASANT—And I.

THIRD PEASANT—And I'm not goin' to be left behind.

TIM.—Then we'll all go instead of havin' others fightin' our battles.

A VOICE—(*Outside.*) Get up there ye lazy divil! Whoa, now, steady! None o' yer pranks! Whoa, there! Get down out o' that Paddy Flynn! How the divil is the mule goin' to stir the weggon an' you in it?

CASS.—(*Looking* L.). Begorra, Tom Considine's mule is stuck in the mud! Come on boys an' give him a hand.

(*Exeunt omnes* L. *Enter* SERGEANT BLAKELY *and the* SOLDIER, R.)

SOLDIER—Quick! Now is our chance! Be careful!

(*They cross to* L., *is. the rear*).

SERG.—Get behind this tree, and wait till they get abreast of us. Are your companions below ?

SOLDIER—Yes, I left three of them there. Take care ! Now is our time !

(*Exeunt* SERGEANT *and* SOLDIER L. *Re-enter* BARNEY, CASSIDY, TIM *and the* PEASANTS, *together with two more of the latter*).

CONSIDINE—Barney O'Reilly divil another load of pikes will I come for if ye can't give us better roads. My ould mule even is kickin' against them, an' when that mule begins to kick, I tell ye he kicks. Have you the pikes ready for us ?

BAR.—I have Tommy, but never mind them just now. Sit down an' rest yourself.

(*One of the new-comers*, FLYNN, *throws himself on the ground*).

CONSIDINE—(*Lighting his pipe*). Look at Paddy Flynn. 'Pon me word he's the laziest man in all Ireland. Whenever he gets the chance he'll lie down an' take a sleep.

CASS.—That may be so Tom, but he's a fine boy to sing a song. Get up Paddy, an' let us have your old favorite.

(FLYNN *Sings*).

CONSIDINE—Paddy me boy, no one can sing that song like yerself. (*Looks* L.). Hi ! What are ye doin' there ? Leave that mule alone ! Leave him alone d'ye hear ! The divil take the fellow, the mule'll kick the head off him ! Whoa, there !

(*Runs out* L.).

CASS.—What is wrong ? Who is it ? Oh be the powers if it is'nt Bootjack !

(*Re-enter* CONSIDINE *with* BEAUJACQUES *a prisoner*.)

CONSIDINE—(*To* BEAUJACQUES.) Who are ye, an' what d'ye mean by ticklin' that mule in the hind legs ?

BEAU.—I not kick de mule in de hind legs !

CASS.—Misther Bootjack, how are ye !

BEAU.—Ah, Monsieur Cassidy, is dat you ! And Monsieur Brannigan, too !

CONSIDINE.—What is it, Micky ?

CASS.—(*Aside*) A poor divil that used to be down at O'Gorman's, an' he's the greatest coward in the world. Begorra, we'll have some fun with him.

BEAU.—Ah, Monsieur Cassidy, you make to me a mistake when you tell it to say "God save de King." Ah, dat God save de King give me plenty trouble.

CASS.—How was that ?

s

BEAU.—Well, when I tell it to Monsieur O'Gorman, God save de King, he cal' me one damfool, an' when I say hurrah for King Billy to de soldier, he want to kill me. Ah, dare is some eting wrong wit dat King.

CONSIDINE.—Micky, what does he mean ?

CASS.—Oh, Tim an' I just played a trick on him, an' it has worked like a charm. (To BEAUJACQUES.) Look here, me friend, ye must have made a mistake. Ye did'nt say God save the King in the right way I'm sure.

BEAU.—Ah, yes, I say it correct, but I not say it any more. When a man she get angry wit me I will say, " to de dayvil wit de King !" and perhaps dat be better.

CASS —(Aside.) Boys, let us have some fun. We'll have a drill with the pikes. Come on every man of ye an' get one in yer hand. (Aloud.) Misther Bootjack, did you ever drill with a pike ?

(All procure pikes.)

BEAU.—Drill wit a pike ! I not know what it is.

CASS.—Well, I'll show ye. Line up there, boys. (All stand in a row. CASSIDY hands a pike to BRAUJACQUES.) Here, take this in yer hand, an' stand over here. (Places him at the end of the row.) Now, when I say "attention" ye must look at me ; now—attention !—that's right ;—shoulder arms—(BEAUJACQUES places the end of the pike on his shoulder in a perpendicular position.) Hold on there Misther Bootjack—why don't ye follow the other boys ?

BEAU—Follow de boys ! Dey are not going away !

CASS —I mean to do as ye see them doin'.

BEAU.—How can I see dem when you say I must look at you ?

CASS.—Ah, I see. I'll have to give ye a lesson all to yerself. Step over here an' we'll have a little practice. Stand right there now, an' when I say right foot, ye must lift yer right, and when it's left foot, lift the left.

BEAU—Left, left. lift de left foot ! What are you talking about ? I not understand.

CASS.—Why, it's very simple. When I say right foot, ye'll lift that one, an' when I say left foot, ye'll lift the other. Try again. Right foot. (BEAU lifts the right and keeps it there.) Left foot.

BEAU—How de dayvil can I lift de left foot ? Dat's all I have for stand on !

CASS.—Arrah, man, put down yer right, an' don't be standin' like a hen on a hot griddle !—That's right. Now, dress up !

BEAU—Eh ?

CASS.—Dress up, I say.

BEAU.—By gosh, I got all my clothes on ! I not put any more dress.

CASS—Oh dear, oh dear, I'll never be able to make a soldier out of ye ! Here, pt . yer pike under yer arm. This way. (Showing him how to do it.) Now when I say " ready" just act as if there was an enemy in front of ye. Pay attention now. Ready !.

(BEAUJACQUES *charges at* CASSIDY, *knocking him over, then runs at the others.*)

ALL.—Hold on there ! Hold on !

CASS.—Who the divil told ye to do that, ye omadhawn !

BEAU.—You tell it to me to do just do same as if de enemy was dere and dat's what I do.

CASS.—Begorra then ye don't need any more teachin' from me, for ye know already how to kill a man without drillin' at all. To the divil with the drill ! Come on boys an' let us have a dance.

(*They dance an Irish reel.*)

CASS.—(*After the dance.*) Oh, boys, we were forgettin' all about our prisoner !

CONS.—A prisoner, Micky !

CASS.—Yes, Tommy ; sure we captured a fellow that was playin the spy, an' we put him into the cabin above, till you'd come up an' take him away with ye.

CONS.—Then let us go up an' bring him down.

(*All go out* R , *with the exception of* BARNEY, DAN, TIM *and* BEAUJACQUES.)

BAR.—Faith the boys 'll be wantin' a load of pikes when they come back I must see about them.

(*Enter* L. SERGEANT BLAKELY *and* THREE SOLDIERS. *The latter level their rifles.*)

BLAKE.—Surrender, in the name of the King !

BEAU.—To de dayvil wit de King ! (*Trembles*).

BLAKE.—What's that you say ?

BEAU.—To de davvil wit de King ! God save de King !- Hurrah for de King ! To de dayvil wit de King !

BLAKE.—(*To* BEAU). I will see that you suffer for this ! (*To* TIM). Where is Dermot O'Gorman ?

TIM—Divil a know I know an' you won't know either !

BLAKE.—We'll see about that, (*Aside to soldiers*). Our informant was positive. We'll take these fellows below and lie in wait for O'Gorman. We have our orders to capture him and it must be done. (*Aloud, to* TIM.) Where are your companions ?

TIM—Gone fishin'. (*Aside*). How the divil did this fellow escape ?

BLAKE.—Ready, men ! Conduct these fellows below. (*To the others*). Fall in there ! March !

(Exeunt L. Enter R. CASSIDY and the rest).

CASS.—There's Blakely, and he has captured the boys we left behind ! Quick, get yer pikes ! *(Each procures a pike).* Now, down on them !

(Exeunt L. Clashing of arms and all re-enter, the soldiers in custody and deprived of their arms. CASSIDY carries the SERGEANT'S sword).

BEAU.—Milles tonneres! Dis is too much for me. I get notting but trouble on his country, and if I stay one day more you can say dat Beaujacques is one grand fou ! To the dayvil wit de King—to de dayvil wit everyting ! Vive la France !

(Runs owt R.).

CASS—*((To BLAKELY.)* So ye thought ye'd get the better of us, eh ?
TIM.—*(Aside to CASS.)* Micky, he was after Captain Dermot to capture him !
CASS.—*(To BLAKELY.)* Oh, ho ! So ye were after bigger game when ye came across us ! Who gave ye the order to capture Dermot O'Gorman ?
BLAKE.—That is my affair.
CASS.—We'll see about that. Boys, take yer prisoners off with ye.

(Enter L. DERMOT and some SOLDIERS.)

CASS.—Oh, here comes Captain Dermot himself !
DERMOT—*(To his men).* Halt ! Cassidy, what means this ? You have taken same prisoners !
CASS.—Faith we did captain, an' rascally prisoners too, for Sergeant Blakely there had been sent out to capture you, but instead he got caught himself.
DERMOT—Sergeant Blakely, you have heard the accusation brought against you ?
BLAKE.—I do, and it is true.
DERMOT—Very good. You have endeavored to effect my capture, but you were merely acting under the orders of your superior. I not only forgive you, but will also repay you for a recent kindly act on your part, and which I, as an Irishman, am bound to requite. Cassidy, restore their arms to these men.
What, captain ! Is this the way ye treat people who want

. . . . —Do as I tell you, Cassidy.
. . . . *aside.)* He has lost his senses. *(Aloud.)* Boys, give them back their guns—Captain Dermot must be obeyed.

(They restore the arms.)

DERMOT.—*(To CASSIDY.)* To whom does that sword belong ?

CASS.—Faith it's the sergeant's !

DERMOT.— Give it to me. (*To* BLAKELY.) Sergeant Blakely, a few days ago some English soldiers captured a few of our Irish people—old men and helpless women and children They were about to ill-use their prisoners when you interfered and drew your sword in defence of the hapless creatures. I wish to express my gratitude for your manly act, and thus I do it. Take back the sword that was drawn in defence of the helpless.

(*Taking the sword.*)

BLAKE.—Captain O'Gorman, you have spoken the truth. This sword has been drawn to protect women and children, but it has also been used against Irish patriots—men such as you have proved yourself to be. I will not be out-done in generosity, and from this moment I cast aside my sword, and shall not take it up again while there is to be found, under the battle flag of Ireland, a soldier as generous and as truly noble as Captain Dermot O'Gorman !

(*Throws aside his sword.* DERMOT *grasps his hand.*)

ACT III.

SCENE—*An* IRISH SENTINEL *discovered walking to and fro.* *Enter*
NUGENT R. *The sentinel halts and salutes.*

NUGENT—Well. Rory, no sign of the enemy ?

SENT.—No, Captain, although a few moments ago I thought I heard a sound of galloping horses, but I must have been wrong, for all is still.

NUGENT—We must be very careful, for the King's troops hold possession of this part of the country. Hist ! What is that !

(*Both listen*)

SENT.—I hear nothing.

NUGENT—I must have been mistaken, but I thought I heard hoof-beats in the distance ! Advance about a hundred yards, and should you hear any suspicious sounds report at once to me.

SENT.—Yes, Captain.

(*Salute and exit L. Enter* DERMOT, R)

NUGENT—Dermot, my boy, I think we shall have to press forward to Limerick without our night's rest.

DERMOT—Why so ?

NUGENT—I may be wrong, but I think that a body of horse is not far from where we stand. I have sent Rory Maguire to reconnoitre, and we shall soon learn whether I am right or wrong.

DERMOT—We are certainly in the midst of danger, but such is the lot of a soldier in time of war. (*Takes papers from his pocket*). Nugent, these are the despatches of which I was speaking this morning.

I now ask you to take charge of them for delivery, into the hands of the governor of Limerick.

NUGENT—*I take charge of them !* Why, man, what do you mean !

DERMOT—I do not know whether or not you will laugh at me, but —Nugent, I am not myself to-night. A presentiment, dark and forbidding hangs over my spirits like a cloud. I feel that some dread fate is about to overtake me.

NUGENT—Tut, tut, man ! You must throw off this feeling of gloom. Trouble of any kind is bad enough when it comes, but its fancied approach is often worse than the evil itself.

DERMOT—I know it, but try as I may I cannot rid myself of the weight which oppresses me. You are aware that Colonel Breckenridge is marching to Limerick !

NUGENT—I am. What of him !

DERMOT—Nothing, but my father is with him. My father, Roger O'Gorman, is now an officer in the army of the King who has sworn the destruction of Irish freedom, and whose guns are even now trained upon the devoted walls of Limerick !

NUGENT—Yes, but even your father's deplorable conduct should not dampen the order of his son, or bring despair to his heart. Cheer up O'Gorman ; matters are not as bad as they might be, and again, there is a chance that your father may see the error of his ways, and repair them.

DERMOT—Yes, but who will guarantee his safety ! Who is it that has said, " Thus far shalt thou go but no farther " ! Ah, Nugent, while my father is aiding our enemies in the siege of Limerick, he may be struck by the hand of death, and loaded with sin, be hurried before his Maker, that God whom he has denied !

NUGENT.—O'Gorman, that God, although just and powerful, is also a forgiving and merciful God ; and who will dare to say that he may not pardon and save the father through the prayer of the son ! Bear like a man this grievous affliction ; chase from your mind the gloom of despondency, and, Dermot O'Gorman, Irishman and patriot, trust in Heaven !

DERMOT —(*Extending his hand.*) Thank you, Nugent ; your words of hope have already removed at least a part of the pain at my heart, and I promise that henceforth I shall be sustained by the thought that my father may yet return to honor and to God.

(*The sound of galloping is heard.*)

NUGENT.—What is that ! A horseman approaching !

(*They look L. The sound ceases.*)

SENT.—(*Outside, at L.*) Who goes there !

HOGAN.—Roderick Hogan

SENT.—Advance and give the countersign.

HOGAN.—Sarsfield !

SENT.—Pass, friend.

(*Enter* Hogan L., *saluting.*)

NUGENT.—Roderick Hogan, by all that's wonderful ! Why, man, I thought you were snug behind the walls of Limerick !

HOGAN—Faith and so I was a short time ago, but I'm now on a night ride of something like twelve miles.

DERMOT—What is the news from Limerick !

HOGAN—News, Captain ! By the sword of Brian the news is great ! Limerick is in a state of siege ; the King's gunners have been battering away at her walls the live-long day, but as sure as my name is Roderick Hogan not a stone has fallen, and the King and his army have retired a full mile so as to be out of range of our guns !

NUGENT—Well done, Limerick !

HOGAN—Aye, faith it was well done, indeed ! The besiegers were compelled to retire, but King William hasn't been idle. We learned this morning that, knowing his weakness in heavy guns, he has sent to Waterford and ordered up a battering train and enough ammunition to carry on the siege for a month. But Captain, those guns will never reach King William !

DERMOT—-How so ! What do you mean !

HOGAN—I mean that there is one who has planned to capture and destroy the battering train !

DERMOT—Good heaven, what a daring venture ! Who is the hero that will attempt such a glorious deed ! There is but one man in Ireland whose brain could conceive the thought and he is—

HOGAN.—The hope of Erin—Patrick Sarsfield !

NUGENT.—Can it be possible that General Sarsfield would dare to attempt this gigantic task !

HOGAN.—Dare to attempt it ! Why, Captain, 'tis as good as done when Sarsfield plans the assault and leads the charge !

DERMOT.—When does he propose to make the attack !

HOGAN.—To-night—perhaps within half an hour, for yonder (*pointing to* R. *in rear*) in fancied security lie the body of troops which accompany the battering train. Sarsfield is approaching at the head of five hundred picked soldiers and he will need them all for the enemy is in force.

NUGENT.—Will the General pass this way !

HOGAN.—The detachment will remain below, but Sarsfield is coming forward with a few of his troopers. Ah, here they come ! (*Looking* L.) Even though 'tis night I can distinguish the white charger that bears the hope and the pride of the nation !

(*Sound of galloping outside.*)

A VOICE.—Halt !

34

(The sound ceases.)

SENT.—Who goes there ?

SARSFIELD.—Patrick Sarsfield.

SENT.—Pass, General.

(*Enter* SARSFIELD L Both captains salute him).

SARSFIELD—Ah, my brave captains I am glad to meet you. Know you aught of the enemy in these parts ?

DERMOT—We have not seen them, General, on our way hither, and, apart from the information conveyed by Corporal Hogan, we know nothing of them.

SARS.—Ah, yes, you refer to the battering train. That must be captured and it shall be. You bear despatches to the Governor of Limerick, captain ?

DERMOT—Yes, general.

SARS. - Then add this to their number ; I have learned that King William has been apprised of our expedition and, in order to frustrate us, has despatched Colonel Breckenridge with reinforcements to the probable scene of action ; but, thanks to our trusty guide, who knows every rod of the country, we shall arrive in time to effect the destruction of the train upon which the King depends for the capture of Limerick, yea, and for the slaughter of the brave fellows who are so nobly defending the town they love so well.

DERMOT—General, may I—may we accompany you and share the danger and the glory of this night's work ?

SARS.—Nay, that cannot be, for upon the despatch which I have given you depends the safety of the gallant fellows under my command, for if help reach us not, our return journey may prove our last (*Turns to* NUGENT.) Captain, I have also a task for you. (*Gives a paper.*) Press forward with all speed to Ballyneety and place this in the hands of Colonel O'Grady.

NUGENT—General, is it your intention to capture the battering train and ammunition for use in the defence of Limerick ?

SARS.—No. Did we but capture it, we should lose it again, for our prize could not be defended against the hosts that would overwhelm us ere we reached the town. No ; we shall apply the match ; we shall destroy both guns and ammunition, and the shock of the explosion will carry dismay to Ireland's enemies and joy to the hearts of the brave defenders of Limerick.

(Moves to L.)

DERMOT—May Heaven grant you victory, General !

SARS.—Aye, may the God of battle strengthen our arms this night for upon the success of our mission depends the fate of Limerick ! Hasten, my friends, to execute your respective tasks and God be with you.

Exit L. *followed by* DERMOT, NUGENT *and* HOGAN. *Enter* R. *an* ENGLISH SOLDIER. *He moves stealthily to* CENTRE *and looks* L.

SOLDIER.—There are but three or four ! Who is it that mounts the white horse ! A person of rank I should say.

(*Sound of footsteps*, R.)

Ah, who comes now !

(*He hides. Enter* R., CASSIDY *and* TIM *in uniform.*)

CASS.—Well, Tim, my boy, I think we'll be off to Limerick very soon. The captain has a whole arm full of despatches an' ordhers for the Governor, an' its very little sleep we'll get to-night an' I'm sorry for it, for I'm as sleepy as a porpoise.

TIM.—Faith an Micky I'm very glad of it, for I don't like the place we're in. Only a few minutes ago I thought I saw something movin' over by the bush, but when I came up to the place I could'nt see anything

CASS.—Indeed an' ye did'nt, for there was nothin' to see. I wonder where the two captains are gone to !

TIM.—I don't know. They were here a few minutes ago talkin' to somebody.

(*The* SOLDIER *in rear lights a wax taper and, affixing it to the point of his bayonet, holds it high in the air.*)

CASS—Ah, Tim, we'll have fine times when we get into Limerick. Nothin' to do all day but fight from mornin' till night ——

TIM—Whisht, Micky ! Did ye hear anything !

CASS.—Not a sound, Tim.

TIM—Faith an' I did.

(*Turns and sees the soldier, who advances and levels his rifle*).

SOLDIER—If you stir a foot I shall fire !

CASS.—Then ye need'nt for sorra a foot we'll stir. (*Aside*). Tim, ye divil, where's yer gun !

SOLDIER—Who is the man you spoke of just now as being the bearer of despatches for the Governor of Limerick !

CASS.—Faith I don't know what yer talkin' about. (*Aside*). Tim, we must get that gun !

SOLDIER—I shall give you just thirty seconds to answer me. Who carries the despatches to Limerick !

CASS.—Begorra I can't hear a word ye say. Speak louder. (*Aside*). Tim, I'll ate me coat if we dont get that gun. Get up there a bit.

(TIM *moves a little to* R.).

SOLDIER—(*To* TIM). Halt, or I fire !

CASS.—Soldier, for the Lord's sake don't kill the boy—he's only a poor half witted idiot !

SOLDIER—Perhaps he has more sense than you possess. (*To* TIM.) Answer me, fellow—your life depends upon it ! Where are the despatches !

TIM.—(*Idiotically.*) Eh !

SOLDIER—Confound the pair of you ! Answer me or you die !

TIM.—Were ye speakin' to me !

SOLDIER.—Quick—I will count five—one—two—

CASS.—Hold on, Misther Soldier, what is it ye want to know ! (*Aside.*) Tim, we're in a tight place, but we'll get that gun !

SOLDIER.—I'll give you another chance. Hurry up—one—two—

CASS.—(*Aside,*) Be ready now Tim, be ready !

SOLDIER.—Three—four—

CASS.—(*Holding up his hand at an imaginary person,* L.) Stop, Paddy ! For God's sake don't kill him like that ! Stop, I tell ye !

(*The* SOLDIER *turns quickly to see whence the danger comes*).

CASS.—Now, Tim, jump on him !

(TIM *rushes upon the* SOLDIER *and snatches the rifle from his hands*).

TIM.—(*Leveling rifle*). Answer me ! Who carries the despatches to Limerick !

(*Mimicking the* SOLDIER).

CASS.—Misther Soldier, the tables are turned on ye. Now it's our turn an' we'll give ye just thirty seconds to answer a question. Who were ye makin' the signal to !

SOLDIER.—You will soon know.

CASS.—Tim, is the thrigger of the gun up !

TIM.—It is Micky.

CASS.—(*To soldier.*) Go on now, answer me ; (*solemnly*) your life depends upon it !

SOLDIER.—Shoot if you will, but let me tell you that others will avenge my death !

CASS.—Shoot ye, is it ! Shoot a man that can't defend himself ! No, Misther Sassenach Soldier, we're too Irish for that ! Tim, me boy, keep him under yer thumb till I find the Captain.

(*About to go out* L. *Sound of marching heard. Looks to* R.) What is that ! The enemy. My God ! Where is Captain O'Gorman !

(*Enter* DERMOT *and* NUGENT L. CASSIDY *addresses* DERMOT.)

Captain, jump on yer horse an' fly for yer life ! The enemy is upon us !

DERMOT—(*Putting his hand to his breast.*) Great Heaven, the despatches ! Sarsfield !

CASS.—Quick, Captain, quick, or it'll be too late !

DERMOT.—(*Taking the despatches from his pocket.*)—Nugent, mount your horse and away with these despatches ! There is time yet to escape !

NUGENT.—And leave you in the hands of the enemy ! Never ! If we must die we shall die together ! (*Draws his sword.*)

DERMOT.—Go, Nugent, for God's sake, Go !

NUGENT.—Not if you stay behind !

DERMOT,—I must stay to put the enemy off the track. Sarsfield's safety and success are worth more than my life !

(*Sound of marching increases in volume.*)

CASS.—Quick, Captain, for Heaven's sake !

NUGENT—(*To Dermot.*) I cannot leave you thus !

DERMOT—You must, for all is lost if the despatches fall into the hands of the enemy ! (*Hands the despatches*). Quick, if you love Ireland and Sarsfield !

NUGENT—Then, in the name of Ireland and Sarsfield I obey, but, Dermot, I will save you yet !

(*Takes the despatches and exit L. Enter* O'GORMAN *and some* SOLDIERS, R.).

O'G.—Surrender, rebels !

DERMOT—(*Aside*). My father ! (*Aloud*). Your numbers are too great for resistance ; we surrender. (*Gives up his sword*).

O'G —(*Aside*). Can it be possible ! My son ! (*To* SOLDIERS). Remove these prisoners and leave me alone with this one.

(*Exeunt soldiers,* TIM *and* CASSIDY, R.).

CASS.—(*To* SOLDIER, *as he goes out*). Take yer dirty paw off me or I'll break yer neck !

O'G.—(*To* DERMOT). Ah, ha, we have met, and sooner than I expected !

DERMOT—Alas, that we should ever meet—thus !

O'G.—You have brought it upon yourself. You defied me ; you followed the dictates of your own stubborn heart, and you should not complain when you find yourself entrapped, with death, a rebel's death, before you !

DERMOT.—I rail not at the fortune of war ; but to know that my father is my persecutor—the persecutor of my gallant countrymen—to see him in the uniform of the enemies of his own country—that is worse than the bitterness of death !

O'G.—Yes, and I shall continue to wear it while there remains a single man clothed in that hated livery. You shall meet the doom of a traitor, for you have been false to me, false to yourself, and false to your King !

DERMOT.—False to my King ? Who is he ?

O'G.—William of Orange.

DERMOT.—William of Orange is not my King ! England does not want him ; gallant Scotland has repudiated and defeated him, and Ireland, noble Ireland, will never bow her unconquored and unconquerable head before him !

O'G.—Then, the blood from the hearts of her sons and daughters shall flow in her valleys and redden her streams, for the sword of William shall remain unsheathed while there lives a man who refuses to acknowledge his supremacy ! But enough of this—I am wasting time.

(Turns to R.)

Corporal Dingley !

(Enter DINGLEY.)

Did you learn anything from the rebels before we arrived ?

DING.—Yes. Major ; I overheard one of them state that a captain was the bearer of despatches for the Governor of Limerick.

O'G.—What captain ?

DING.—I didn't hear the name, sir.

O'G.—Anything else ?

DING.—When I arrived some person was in the act of mounting his horse, but I was too late to catch a glimpse of his face.

O'G.—That will do. You may retire.

Exit DINGLEY R.)

DERMOT.—*(Aside)* I thank God that he did not see his face !

O'G.—*(To DERMOT.)* I have only a few questions to ask but they are of great import. Who is the bearer of the despatches in question ?

DERMOT—I refuse to answer.

O'G.—Have you any knowledge of such despatches ?

DERMOT—I know that they exist.

O'G.—And you refuse to name the bearer ?

DERMOT.—Yes, I refuse.

O'G.—Perhaps you are the man !

DERMOT—They were placed in my hands one hour ago.

O'G.—Then I order you to produce them !

DERMOT—And I refuse to do so.

O'G.—Well, we shall try a little force.

(Steps to R.)

Corporal Dingley !

Enter DINGLEY.

DERMOT—*(Aside.)* I must gain time ! I must delay the pursuit !

O'G.—(*To* DINGLEY).   Bring in two of your men and a stout rope.

(DINGLEY *salutes and exit* R.).

DERMOT—(*Aside*).   What is he about to do ?

O'G.—(*To* DERMOT).   Now for another question : What do you know of Sarsfield's plan to capture a battering train which is hastening .to the King's aid ?

DERMOT—Nothing.

O'G—Speak the truth or you may compel me to take extreme measures !

DERMOT—I speak the truth ; I know nothing of Sarsfield's plans except that which shall remain locked in my breast !

O'G.—Ha—we shall see.   Now, about this man who was about to ride away when yonder corporal arrived here.   Who is he ?

DERMOT.—A soldier of Ireland !

O'G —A very satisfactory answer.

(*Enter* DINGLEY *and two soldiers with a rope.*)

Men, bind the prisoner's arms.

DERMOT.—What !   You order your slaves to thus degrade an O'Gorman !

O'G Yes, a rebel O'Gorman deserves such treatment.   Men, obey me !

(SOLDIERS *seize and bind* DERMOT'S *arms.*)

Corporal, take the prisoner outside and search him.

Exeunt SOLDIERS *and* DERMOT, R.

DERMOT.—(*To* O'GORMAN *as he goes out*)   To what unmanly deeds will not ungoverned passion lead a man !

O'G.—(*Solus.*)   What a stubborn spirit and yet how lordly !   When I listen to his lofty sentiments and meet the bold and penetrating glance of his eyes I feel humbled, and I have to confess that he, a captive, is greater than I.   But he must bend to my will.   He shall reveal his knowledge of Sarsfield's plan of action, for his presence in this place is a proof that he possesses such knowledge.   We are working in th' dark. We know nothing of Sarsfield's whereabouts, nor are we aware of the location of the battering train, without which we cannot conquer Limerick.

(*Stops and picks up a piece of paper.*)

Ha !   What is this !   (*Reads.*)   " *I have arranged that Colonel O'Grady shall meet us after the destruction of the battering train, the success of which feat shall be made patent to you by means of one of the grandest displays of fireworks you have ever seen.   The explosion of one hundred tons of the enemy's powder will teach William and his followers that Limerick's defenders are awake and watchful.— 'Sarsfield.*"   Where did this come from ? and to whom was it addressed ? We shall learn.

(Steps to R.).

What can be the cause of Dingley's delay?

(Looks out R at rear. Enter CASSIDY R. *in front, with rifle).*

CASS.—*(Moving cautiously).* Begorra I've got away from the divils, an' if I don't bring a hornet's nest around that thraitor's head ye can call me a Rooshian! Yes, Masther Dermot alanna, ye'll not be very long in the hands of yer ould divil of a father, if Micky Cassidy can help ye, an' Micky Cassidy can an' will!

(Exit CASS. L. *Enter A* SOLDIER R. *carrying his rifle.)*

SOLDIER.—Major, one of the prisoners has escaped!

O'G.—Then pursue him, blockhead, and kill him if necessary.

(Exit SOLDIER L. *a shot is heard followed by a second.)*

CASS.—*(Outside.)*—Bad manners to ye! Sure ye might know that ye'd get hurt if ye interfered with Micky Cassidy's business!

(Re-enter SOLDIER *wounded*)

O'G.—Ha, ha! Wounded, eh? Apprise Captain Hobson of the escape and tell him to order an immediate pursuit by way of the river bank.

(Exit SOLDIER R. *Re-enter* DINGLEY *and* DERMOT, *the latter's coat in disorder*)

O'G.—Well, Corporal?

DING.—I have been unable to find any papers on the prisoner, and my search has revealed nothing but this. *(Hands a locket to* O'GORMAN).

O'G.—You may retire.

(Exit DINGLEY.*)*

O'G.—*(To* DERMOT.*)* The picture of your forlorn sweetheart, I suppose! *(Opens locket*) Ah! The face of my dead wife!

DERMOT—Yes, the picture of that sainted woman, my mother, who, even now, kneels before the throne of God and beseeches Him to spare her husband!

O'G,—*(Aside.)* Away with this weakness! He must obey or die!

(Places locket in his pocket.)

(Aloud.) To whom did you give the despatches?

DERMOT—To one who will carry them to their destination.

O'G.—Unhappy boy, do you know the fate your obstinacy will bring upon you? Can you not realize the danger in which you stand?

DERMOT.—I know that my life is in your hands.

O'G.—And know you not that my duty to my King will compel me to take that life if you persist in your determination to withhold the information I desire?

DERMOT.—I am aware that you can and may order your slaves to destroy me, but if I had a thousand lives you might kill me a thousand times ere I should prove faithless to Sarsfield or to Ireland which is my King!

O'G.—Well, since threats cannot weaken you we shall see what torture may do!

(*Moves to R.*)

DERMOT.—Father, you cannot mean it! Torture!

O'G.—Yes, torture! A stubborn will may remain unshaken until the agonizing pains of the body compel obedience!

DERMOT—Father, the most violent bodily pain will never compel my tongue to blacken my soul with the crime of treason to my country. I fear not torture by the rack or the sword, but—O God! my soul recoils at the horrible thought that the author of my being should contemplate, even for a moment, such a terrible crime against nature! Father, has all remembrance of earlier and happier days been blotted from your mind! Can you not recall the first time that you imprinted on my forehead a fatherly kiss! Do you not still feel the clinging arms of my mother about your neck—her tender caress? Can you not hear the faint but sweet echo of her voice as she whispered in your ear " Roger, I thank God for having given us a son," ? And later, when dark clouds overshadowed our home, did not your dying wife use her tongue, so soon to be stilled forever, in beseeching you to spare that son ? Oh father, you cannot have forgotten !

O'G.—(*Aside*). I am moved in spite of myself but he shall not unman me! (*Aloud*). Speak no more of the past. 'Tis the present and the future with which I have to do.

DERMOT.—Then let not that future be blasted by the ghost of a heinous crime. Bring to your aid the moral courage which I know you possess. Awaken your slumbering but really noble soul. Open again that locket and gaze on the pictured face of one you loved who is now in the cold embrace of the grave ; yes, but whose spirit looks down from the mystic heavens, hoping, praying, entreating you to listen to the voice of your conscience—the voice of your heart! Renounce the cause you espoused in a moment of passion—in a spirit of revenge ! Abandon the people with whom you are leagued. Fly with me, and in the ranks of the patriot army, strike for God and for Ireland !

O'G.—(*Aside*.) So young and yet so noble ! Must he die ? (*Aloud.*) My son—yes, I will again call you my son, for your voice, as I now hear it, brings back to my ear another voice long since hushed by death, the recollection of which gives me both pleasure and pain, for I cannot forget that it was your mother who neutralized and finally destroyed the effect of my teaching. My son, I wish to save you, and I can and will on one condition.

DERMOT.—And that is —— ?

O'G.—To give a truthful answer to a question which I will put to you.

DERMOT—If I answer it I will do so truthfully, for although you have held and still hold opinions abhorrent to me, yet I must say that you have ever taught me to shun the language of falsehood ; but if the reply involves treason to the Irish cause then I shall remain dumb.

O'G.—Very good ; here is the question : By what road does Sarsfield march to-night ? (*A pause.*) Ah, you refuse to answer !

DERMOT—Yes, for the reason already given.

O'G.—Was Sarsfield here this night ?

DERMOT—I have already stated that such questions shall receive no answer.

O'G —(*Producing Sarsfield's note.*) Then look at this !

(DERMOT *reads and starts when he reaches the signature.*)

O'G.—To whom was that note addressed ?

DERMOT—I know not.

O'G.—Was it intended for you ?

DERMOT—It was not.

O'G.—Has it been in your possession ?

DERMOT—I never saw it until this moment.

O'G.—Very good. Now I shall tell you what I infer from the note and your refusal to answer my question, and it is this : that Sarsfield himself has been here and dropped this precious piece of paper, or, his messenger has done so. In either case you have been made acquainted with his plans, and you shall be compelled to reveal the knowledge you possess.

DERMOT—Father, I——

O'G.—Not a word ! I would have saved you. Your appeal had softened me, but now duty drives out mercy and there remains nothing for you but obedience or death. Dingley !

(*Moves to R. Enter DINGLEY.*)

(*To DINGLEY.*) Remove the prisoner and send the other to me.

DERMOT—(*At R.*) Father, hear me——

O'G.—(*Loudly.*) Corporal Dingley, remove the prisoner !

(*Exeunt DINGLEY and DERMOT.*)

O'G.—What means the struggle that is raging within my breast ? Is it my better self fighting with the devil that has possessed me for many years ? Why have the words and the voice of my son so moved me ? Oh, why has fate decided that we should meet ! Why was he not killed in battle ? Then he would lie in the grave of a soldier—of one who had fought and died for his country ! But now, now an ignoble death awaits him—the death of a rebel ! A rebel ? Ah, Dermot, you are still my son, and I am your father ! Can I forget that ? No ; I must at least save your life !

(Enter TIM.)

TIM.—*(Aside.)* What the divil does he want me for ?

O'G.—*(Giving* TIM *the note)*. Read this !

TIM.—Begorra I've left me glasses behind me but I think I can manage it. *(Reads a portion of the note)*. *(Aloud)*. More power to his elbow ! *(Reads another portion)*. That's what I call spunk ! *" The explosion of a hundred tons of the enemy's powdher'll teach William an' his followers "*—faith he should have said blackguards !— *" will teach William an' his followers that Limerick's defenders are awake an' watchful."* *(Aside)*. Yes an' when they have taken the lesson to heart may the divil fly away with them ! '

O'G.—*(Taking the note)*. Well, what does it mean ?

TIM.—Faith it means that yer goin' to be short of powdher very soon.

O'G.—Was Sarsfield here to-night ?—Speak the truth or your life shall pay the forfeit !

TIM.—*(Aside)*. What the divil will I say ? Bad luck to it but I'm in a nice fix ! *(Aloud)*. No, Sarsfield was'n't here to-night or any other night.

O'G.—Brannigan, owing to the fact that you were once in my service I feel disposed to save your life, although death is the fate of a captured rebel !

TIM.—You are very kind Misther O'Gorman.

O'G.—If you speak the truth and the whole truth, you shall leave here a free man.

TIM.—Well, Misther O'Gorman, jokin' aside, I'd be willin' to tell a lot o' truth for such a reward. *(Aside.)* Begorra he'll hear more lies than he ever heard in his life before.

O.'G.—Very good ; you are a very sensible fellow, and should the information you will give prove to be correct, you shall receive even more than your liberty.

TIM.—Fire away then,——I'm not above makin' something out of the misfortunes of me friends. Go on—I'm ready to answer.

O.G.—Do you know anything of Sarsfield's plans for the attack on the Royal troops guarding the battering train ?

TIM.—*(Aside.)* Divil a thing I know, but that does'nt make any difference. *(Aloud.)* Well, I don't know much, but I've heard a thing or two.

O.'G.—Do you know which road he will follow ?

TIM.—Begorra ye may be sure that Sarsfield's the man to take the shortest cut he can find.

O.'G.—No evasion ! I want you to tell what you know !

TIM.—Well ye see I did'nt think ye'd ask me to betray me Gineral, an' I don't think I can bring myself to do it. *(Aside)* Faith I think that Sarsfield is about blowin' up that powdher by this time, an' I'll be safe in tellin' something that'll keep this fellow where he is till the harm's done.

O'G.—What means this hesitation?

TIM.—I wasn't hesitatin', but it has just struck me that you'll put an end to me if I don't answer, an' if I do, I'll have to leave Ireland, for if the boys found out what I had done they'd cut me to pieces, an' it's as broad as it's long no matter what I do.

O'G.—I shall take care that your information goes not beyond myself. You may rest easy on that point.

TIM.—Well then—are ye sure there's no one listenin'?

(*Moves closer to* O'GORMAN.)

O'G.—Quite sure. We are alone.

TIM.—Oh, what am I about to do! Betray them that never harmed me!

O'G.—(*Becon . . . ed.*) Do not think of others! Remember that you are in my ' ' '

TIM.—Yes, God foigive me! that's me only excuse. Well, life is sweet an' I'm goin' ve m . General Sarsfield is goin' to take the very road we're on this . . . . te!

O'G.—How do you know?

TIM.—Because we were waitin' here to join him.

O'G.—Ah, ha! You may now retire, and when the right time comes you shall have your liberty and your reward.

TIM.—(*Aside, while he moves to* R.) Begorra I have him stuffed up to the neck! Tim, me boy, ye'd make a fine divil's advocate!

(*Exit* R.)

O'G —Now my way is clear! Colonel Breckenridge shall be made to believe that Dermot has given the information I possess, and thus I shall save my son! Corporal Dingley!

(*Enter* DINGLEY R.)

Send the other prisoner to me.

(*Exit* DINGLEY.)

Yes, I shall inform the Colonel that under a threat of torture my son weakened and confessed. He will never discover the truth for I shall bind him to secrecy.

(*Enter* DERMOT R.)

DERMOT—Have I been called to hear my sentence?

O'G.—No my son, no. (*Aside.*) I must be careful not to betray myself. (*Aloud.*) We have decided to remain here for some time,—an hour, perhaps, and in the meantime nothing will be done as regards yourself.

DERMOT—Father, what is the meaning of your changed demeanor

towards me ! You look as you used to do in the far-off happy past !
You are joyous ! You are ——

O'G.—Hush ! Someone comes.

(Enter COL. BROCKENBRIDGE *R.)*

COLONEL—What, Major ! Your son a prisoner ?

O'G.—*(Aside to* COL.). Yes I have had wonderful luck. Let us
retire and I shall acquaint you with what has transpired.

(Exeunt COL. *and* O'GORMAN *R. Enter a* SENTINEL, *R. in rear who
walks to and fro).*

DERMOT—What can have made such a change in my father ? A few
minutes ago his ferocity led me to believe that my end was near at hand,
but now all seems changed.

(The SENTINEL, *as he walks from side to side, disappears for a few
moments each time he reaches the wings, and while he is thus off
the scene,* NUGENT'S *head appears through an opening in the stage
floor).*

NUGENT—Dermot, is the coast clear ?

DERMOT—Good heaven, Nugent ! Where have you come from ?

NUGENT—*(Emerging from below).* I'll tell you in a minute.

DERMOT—Rash fellow, why do you thus expose yourself to danger ?

NUGENT—To save my friend !

DERMOT—Quick—step this way ! The guard will pass in a moment.

(Enter SENTINEL *who walks across and disappears through the opposite
side.)*

DERMOT—Nugent, what is the meaning of this ? Where are the
despatches ?

NUGENT—Safe on the road to Limerick !

DERMOT—How ? I do not understand.

NUGENT.—They are in the hands of that faithful fellow, Cassidy,
who escaped from this place for the purpose of informing Colonel O'Grady
of your capture. He overtook me on the road to Ballyneety, and something occurred which enabled me to prevail upon him to proceed to Limerick. Who comes now ?

DERMOT.—It is only the sentinel. Step aside.

(Enter SENTINEL *as before and exit the opposite side.)*

NUGENT.—Ere I had gone a mile from this place Cassidy overtook
me, and while conversing we heard the tramp of a large body of men.
We reconnoitred, and to our intense surprise and delight found them to
be a regiment of infantry under the gallant O'Grady, who, knowing of
Sarsfield's daring scheme, decided to act without waiting for orders and
hasten to the assistance of his chief. The moment he heard my news he
decided to march hither and give battle to the force under the command

of Colonel Breckenridge, and he is now advancing as fast as his troops can run.

DERMOT.—My brave and true friend, I thank you for your zeal in my behalf, and I should be ungrateful indeed if I allowed you to remain here another minute. Breckenridge or my father ——

NUGENT.—Your father! Is he here?

DERMOT.—Yes, he is my captor, and I am glad of it, for I feel that my captivity will prove a blessing in disguise. But we are wasting precious time! Escape the way you came and God bless you.

NUGENT—Not a foot shall I move unless you come with me!

DERMOT—No, Nugent, I shall not go. My place is here, for something tells me that my father's heart has softened, and should I leave him now, my fondest hope would surely be shattered.

NUGENT—But your life is in danger! Even should your father desire to save you, Colonel Breckenridge, his superior, would not consent! Quick! Fly with me! Somebody comes.

(Endeavors to drag DERMOT with him.)

DERMOT—Desist, Nugent, desist, and save yourself! Quick! for heaven's sake!

NUGENT—No! If necessary I shall fight and die with you, but leave you—never!

DERMOT—Do not speak of fighting, for I could not aid you—I am without a sword!

NUGENT—But I have mine, and it shall not be idle while I have a friend to defend!

Draws his sword and steps between DERMOT and R. Enter O'GORMAN R.

O'G.—*(Placing his hand on his sword.)* Harry Nugent! How came you here!

DERMOT—Father, at the risk of his life he came here to save me. Let him depart.

O'G.—That I cannot do. Nugent, you are my prisoner!

NUGENT—If any other than you had spoken such words, I would answer him with a thrust, but I cannot draw my sword against the father of Dermot O'Gorman!

DERMOT—Father, hear me! Do not imperil the life of the friend who has tried to save mine! Let him depart in safety.

(Drops on one knee.)

Here on my knees I beseech, I implore you to release him!

O'G.—Rise. *(To Nugent.)* Young man, how did you come here?

NUGENT—By a secret underground passage one outlet of which is here. *(Pointing to the spot.)*

O'G,—Then use that passage now. You are free—for Dermot's sake ! Go !

NUGENT—I thank you, Major O'Gorman, but I will not go and leave Dermot behind !

O'G.—(*After a moment's reflection.*) Dermot, follow your friend.

DERMOT—(*Excitedly.*) Father, come with us ! Heaven has granted my prayer and given you back to me——

O'G.—No ; duty shall keep me here.

DERMOT—Then my duty is plain ; I shall remain by your side. Nugent, my dear friend, go !

O'G.—Yes, go. I shall answer for Dermot's safety.

NUGENT.—If I were sure ——

O.'G.—I have promised. Go, ere it is too late !

DERMOT.—Harry, for my sake listen to my father !

NUGENT.—Major O'Gorman, I trust you. Dermot, I obey.

(Exit by means of the trap-door.)

DERMOT —Father, I thank you.

O.'G.—Then show your gratitude by following the instructions I will now give you. If Colonel Breckenridge questions you concerning Sarsfield's movements, tell him that you cannot answer,—that you have told me all, and that you will tell it to no other. Do you understand !

DERMOT.—Tell him that I have told you all ! What do you mean ?

O.'G.—This is the first time in your life that I have asked you to speak falsely, but now you must obey me !

DERMOT.—But I have told you nothing !

O.'G.—Never mind—promise !

DERMOT.—Yes, I promise not to answer.

(Enter Col. Breckenridge, R.)

COL.—(*Aside, to* O'GORMAN.) O'Gorman, a scout has just come in ; he informs me that a body of Irish infantry is approaching and that their number exceeds a thousand, while Sarsfield has but five hundred, and they are cavalry, not infantry. What does it mean ?

O'G.—I cannot tell. Perhaps the scout is mistaken !

COL.—No ; he is quite positive. However, our men are ready, and whatever the enemy turn out to be, they shall get a warm reception.

(Enter DINGLEY R).

DING.—Colonel, Captain Dickson wishes to know if he will advance a few hundred yards.

COL.—I will see him myself.

(Exeunt COLONEL and DINGLEY R.).

DERMOT—Father, now that you know that Irish troops are approach-ing I will tell you that they are not Sarsfield's men, for Sarsfield is several miles distant, and you will not meet his troops to-night.

48

O'G.—Not meet them to-night ?
DERMOT—No, but more than this I cannot tell.
O'G.—Do you mean to say that Sarsfield will not come this way ?
DERMOT—No, he will not come.
O'G.—Then that scoundrel Brannigan has spoken falsely ! He it was who told me of Sarsfield's route.

(Re-enter COLONEL).

COL.—There is no sign of the enemy yet, O'Gorman.
O'G.—Colonel, I have been misinformed—we have been betrayed ! Sarsfield will not march this way ! The scoundrel who gave the lying information—
COL.—The scoundrel who gave the information ! Does he not stand there ? Is he not your son ?
O'G.—(*Aside*.) Good heaven ! What have I said ?
COL.—Speak ! Does not the traitor stand there in the person of Dermot O'Gorman !

(A vivid light is seen followed by a sound as of an explosion.)
COL.—Great God ! What can that mean ?
DERMOT—I can tell you Colonel Breckenridge ! It means that the gallant Sarsfield has accomplished his purpose, and that Limerick, brave old Limerick is saved !
COL.—(*Stepping to R.*)
Corporal Dingley !

(Enter DINGLEY.)

Remove the prisoner, prepare him for execution, and send a squad here immediately !
O'G.—Breckenridge, what are you about to do ?
COL.—My duty.—Corporal, obey my order ! ·
DERMOT—Father, the blow has fallen !

(Exeunt DERMOT *and* DINGLEY.)

O.'G.—Oh, Dermot, Dermot !—Colonel, for God's sake revoke your order ! My son is innocent—the other prisoner is the guilty one !
COL.—Major O'Gorman, is it manly to thus throw blame upon another even to save a son ?
O.'G.—He is innocent—I swear it ! In my endeavor to save him I gave him credit for information obtained from another ——
COL.—Major, what means this change of sentiment towards your son ? But a short time ago you were more determined upon his death than I—an English soldier. ·
O.'G.—Yes, but my eyes have since been opened to the enormity of my sin. Spare him, spare him ! He is innocent !
COL.—Innocent ! He is a rebel—a follower of that Sarsfield who

has, this moment, destroyed our hope of capturing Limerick ! Speak no more—he shall die !

(*Enter* DINGLEY, *four* SOLDIERS *and* DERMOT, *the latter blindfolded and his arms bound to his sides.* DINGLEY *places* DERMOT *back to* R., *while the* SOLDIERS *line up at* L *, facing him.*)

DERMOT.—Father, I cannot see. Where are you ?

O.'G.—Oh, God ! My son, my son !

DERMOT—Father, do not grieve for me. I die for my country. Tell me, quick, promise that you will grant my last request—to renounce allegiance to the enemy of our country !

O'G —No, no, not that ! 'Tis your love for your country that has brought 'his doom upon you, and now I shall live for revenge upon those who have led you astray—revenge upon their hated country !

DERMOT—Father ! ——

COL.—Major O'Gorman, you may retire. I understand your feelings, but duty forces me to extreme measures.

O'G.—(*To* COLONEL). Will nothing move you to alter your decree ?

COL.—No My duty forbids it.

O'G.—(*Turning away to* R.). My God ! He is lost ! Lost !

COL.—Corporal Dingley, proceed.

DING.—(*To the* FOUR SOLDIERS.) Attention ! Present arms !—One—two——

(O'GORMAN *runs forward and throws his arms around* DERMOT'S *neck.*)

O'G.—Dermot, we shall die together! (*To the* SOLDIERS.) Quick ! Put an end to this agony !

COL.—(*To* SOLDIERS.) Hold ? (*Aside.*) I could see the son die, unmoved, but my old friend's anguish is too much for me. (*Aloud.*) Corporal, the execution will not take place at present. You may retire.

(DINGLEY *salutes.*)

DING.—(*To* SOLDIERS.) Attention ! Shoulder arms ! Left wheel ! Quick march !

(*Exeunt* DINGLEY *and* SOLDIERS.

O'G.—(*Stepping forward.*) Colonel, I cannot thank you——

COL.—Not a word ! It may cost me my colonelcy, but—we were boys together !

(*Extends his hand. Several shots heard, and clashing of steel.*) Ha ! What is that ?

(*Enter* DINGLEY.)

DING.—Colonel, the Irish have arrived and begun the attack. (*Exit.*)

COL.—Quick, Major, follow me !

O'G.—My son !

COL.—He is safe here.

O'G.—But he is bound ! I will release him !

COL.—You have not time. Quick, follow me !

(Exeunt Col. and O'G.)

DERMOT—The clash of arms ! Our gallant fellows have arrived !
(Endeavors to release himself.)

Father, release me ! He is gone ! I am alone and helpless while the battle rages !

(Shots and clashing of arms.)

Father, father, where are you ? O God ! will no one undo these cords ?

(A loud cheer without)

Ha ! That is an Irish cheer !

(Struggles to free himself. Enter R. Two English Soldiers who proceed to load their rifles.)

FIRST SOLDIER—I say Dave, the fight's going against us ! Curse those wild Irishmen !

SECOND SOLDIER—Yes, you're right, but they'll get another pill from me before it's over ! *(Sees Dermot.)* Hello ! What have we here ! *(To Dermot.)* I say, green-coat, how did you get here ? Bill, let us give the fellow a dose to finish him !

(Levels his rifle at Dermot.)

FIRST SOLDIER—What are you doing ? Going to kill a blind man !

(Strikes the barrel of the rifle)

You ought to be ashamed of yourself ! Let us get out of here and fight men with arms !

O'G.—*(Outside)*—Close up there Captain Dickson !

FIRST SOLDIER—There's the Major—come on !

(Exeunt Soldier R)

DERMOT—My father's voice ! He may be killed while fighting the friends of his country ! O God ! do not take him now ! .

NUGENT—*(Outside)*. The steel, boys ! Nothing but the steel ! charge !

(Loud clashing of weapons and more shots).

DERMOT—That is Nugent ! *(Calls).* Nugent ! Nugent !——Ah ! he cannot hear me ! O God ! will I never be free !

(Tries to break the cords. Enter Nugent sword in hand).

NUGENT—Thank God, I am in time !

(*Removes the bandage from* DERMOT's *eyes and cuts the cords with his sword*).

DERMOT.—Again my preserver !

NUGENT.—Quick, Dermot, take this sword and follow me !

(*Hands him a sword which he takes from his scabbard.*)

DERMOT.— One moment, Nugent ! Is my father near at hand ?

NUGENT.—He is. Colonel O'Grady has called upon him to surrender, but he refuses to do so. Hurry, you may save him !

(*Exeunt R. Enter* TIM, R., *in rear.*)

TIM.—Bad luck to the divils, I've got away from them ! Where'll I find a gun or something to fight with ! ·

(*Looks around and discovers a pike.*)

Begorra it's not much of a pike, but it'll do till I get a better one !

(*Shots and noise outside.*)

Now is yer time, Tim, me boy ! Into the fight with ye !

(*Exit R. in front. Re-enter the* TWO ENGLISH SOLDIERS R., *in rear.*)

FIRST SOLDIER.—(*Facing R.*) We're caught like rats in a trap, but we'll sell our lives dearly ! Dave, shoot the first that attempts to enter !

SECOND SOLDIER.—I've got enough of shootin' for to-night. You can do as you please, but I'm going to try to get out of here !

FIRST SOLDIER.—Stand, man, and make a fight for it !

SECOND SOLDIER—I tell you I won't ! Did'nt you see the Colonel fall ?

FIRST SOLDIER—No ; is he killed ?

SECOND SOLDIER—Yes, shot through the head ! Two or three hundred of our fellows have surrendered already, and you may be sure the game is up. (*Looks L.*) What's this ? An opening ! Bill, come here, quick ! We can escape this way !

(*Exeunt L. Enter R. Two* IRISH SOLDIERS).

FIRST SOLDIER—Faith we've thrashed them pretty well this time !

SECOND SOLDIER—Yes, their Colonel is killed, and what's left of them have surrendered. Sure they could'nt do anything else, when Major O'Gorman ordered them to give up. I wonder if poor Captain Dermot is badly hurt ?

FIRST SOLDIER—I fear he is.

(*Enter* TIM R. *in rear*).

TIM.—Where's Captain Dermot ? Is it true that he's wounded ?

FIRST SOLDIER—Faith I'm sorry to say it is. His old rascal of a father was surrounded but would'nt give up He fought like a tiger, and had already struck down several of our men when suddenly Captain

Dermot ran up. He saw his father's peril and cried out "Spare, my father !" and then jumped right in front of him so quickly that he received in his breast a bullet intended for the Major.

TIM.—Oh, my God ! He has given his life to save his father ! Where is he ? Tell me, quick !

FIRST SOLDIER.—They're bringing him here. Hush ! Here they come !

(*Enter* TWO SOLDIERS *carrying* DERMOT *on a litter, and followed by* O'GORMAN *and* NUGENT. *The* SOLDIERS *lay their burden on the floor*)

O.'G.—(*On his knees and supporting* DERMOT'S *head.*) Dermot, Dermot, my boy, speak to me ! Oh, God, he has given his life for his wretched father ! Dermot ! Dermot !

DERMOT.—Ah, it is you, father ! I am so glad that you are safe. Hold my hand—I feel weak.

O.'G.—Would to God that I could suffer in your stead ! Oh, Dermot, why did you save me ?

DERMOT.—That you might live to repent—to become what you once were—what you are still at heart, a believer.

O.'G.—Then you have won—you have conquered me !   Yes, my son, your God is once again and forever my God ! .

DERMOT.—I thank Heaven for this ! Father, there is one thing more—your hatred for your country ——

O.'G.—Is washed away by the blood you have shed for me !

DERMOT.—Ah, now , can die content !

O.'G.—Dermot, Dermot, do not speak of death ! You cannot—you must not die ! No, no ! God, who has inspired you to save me, body and soul, will not ask this sacrifice.

DERMOT—But, father, I feel that I am dying. Tell me that you will submit—console me with the knowledge that you will bow to the will of Heaven !

O'G.—Oh, 'tis hard—'tis almost beyond my strength, but—yes, Dermot, I submit !

DERMOT—Ah, 'tis well ! Father, I have often acted contrary to your wishes—in this I obeyed my conscience, still I have given you pain. Tell me now that you forgive me !

O'G.—Forgive you, my martyred son ! Oh Dermot, you scourge me !

DERMOT—Ah, I see the tears in your eyes ! You weep—you who were once our enemy, but now, thank God, a soldier of Ireland !—Ah, my sight grows dim—I can no longer see your face—all is darkness— put your arms around me—that I may know you are near me—my father—Sarsfield—Ireland—

(*Lies inert in* O'GORMAN'S *arms.*)

O'G.—My God! He is dead! My boy, my bright-souled boy, is dead!

NUGENT—(*On one knee and looking into* DERMOT's *face.*) No, Major, he has only fainted!

(*Enter the* SURGEON.)

Ah, thank Heaven, here is the surgeon!

SURGEON—What have we here! Ah, ha, Dermot O'Gorman wounded! (*Recognizes* O'GORMAN.) What, O'Gorman! Your son!

O'G.—Yes; to save my life he has given his own!

SURGEON—Oh, I hope it is not so bad as that! Allow me.

(*Takes* O'GORMAN's *place the latter moving to the right.*)

O'G.—(*While the surgeon examines the wound.*) O merciful God, save my son! Give him back—restore him to me, and grant that, one day, I may be worthy to stand by his side in the sacred cause of our country!

SURGEON—(*Rising, and laying his hand on* O'GORMAN's *shoulder.*) Cheer up, O'Gorman. The wound is not mortal. Your son will live!

O'G.—He will live! My boy will live! (*Falls on his knees.*) O merciful and powerful God, I thank Thee!

DERMOT—(*Opening his eyes and putting his arm around* O'GORMAN's *neck.*) Father!

ACT IV.

SCENE—The Walls of Limerick. *An Irish flag on a pole at centre.* TIM *and* CASSIDY *discovered looking in the direction of the enemy.*

CASS.—I can't discover a sign of any movement among the enemy, Tim. I wondher what they're about! Faith, it's over two blessed hours since we had a shot from them!

TIM.—Micky, we'll hear from them again, never fear, for it's when the divils are quietest that they're doin' the most harm.

CASS.—Begorra they haven't been very quiet for the 'ast two weeks an' they've done plenty of mischief. I overheard Genera. Sarsfield himself sayin' that he was afraid the walls would'nt stand much more battherin'.

TIM.—Never you mind Micky, even if the walls crumble to dust, for ye may be sure that that same Sarsfield has more ways than one of buttherin' the enemy's pancakes.

CASS.—I don't doubt it Tim; I don't doubt it. Oh, it just struck me now—did ye go up to see how Captain Dermot was gettin' along this mornin'!

TIM.—I did, an' he's doin' splendid. He's a bit weak yet, of course, but in spite of it did'nt he want to get up yesterday, when he heard the heavy cannonadin', but his father wouldn't hear of it. Is n't it a wondherful change that's come over Roger O'Gorman ?

CASS.—Yes, I never saw the like of it. He won't stay away a minute from his son's bedside. Yesterday when I ran in to see how things were goin' I saw Dermot fast asleep ; his father was kneelin' by the bed with his son's hand clasped in his, while every minute his chest 'd heave an' the tears rain down his face. Tim, when I see a strong, stern man like O'Gorman weepin' it ates the heart out of me !

TIM.—I believe ye, Micky, but then it's a good sign, for it shows that his heart is at last in the right place. Yes, thanks be to God, the past fortnight has done wondhers for Roger O'Gorman.

CASS.—(Looking off rear.) Tim ! Tim ! D'ye see the horseman gallopin' across from the enemy's lines ?

TIM.—Faith I do. What's the meaning of it ?

CASS.—An' there's something flyin' in the air behind him. (Shades his eyes with his hand.) Begorra, if it is'nt a white flag—a flag of truce ! (Points R.) Look ! The boys below see him, too. Let us go down—we're not under ordhers yet.

(Exeunt R. Enter L. DERMOT and O'GORMAN, the former leaning on O'GORMAN's arm. The latter is dressed as a civilian.)

DERMOT.—Ah, it is good to be out to-day, and already I feel the enlivening effect of the fresh morning air.

O.'G.—Yes, my boy, it will do you good, but you must not get too much of it ; and above all you shall have to give up the idea of returning to your duty, at least for the present.

DERMOT.—But I am now quite strong and it really retards my recovery to hear the roar of the guns, and to know that my brave companions are fighting for liberty, while my post in the ranks is vacant.

O.G.—Dermot, it shall no longer be so ; a substitute shall be found !

DERMOT.—A substitute ?

O.'G.—Yes, for I shall take your place in the ranks of Limerick's defenders !

DERMOT. — (Gladly.) You, father !

O.'G.—Yes, my boy. I am now the Roger O'Gorman you knew in your childhood. The dark years of the past are to me a hideous nightmare which I desire to forget,—which I never wish to recall, except as a contrast to what I am now—to what I shall be in the future—(aside)— when, with the help of Heaven, I shall render myself worthy of being called the father of Dermot O'Gorman !

(Enter NUGENT L.)

NUGENT.—Major O'Gorman ! Dermot ! How glad I am to see you once again by the walls of Limerick ! Upon my word you are looking almost as strong as ever !

DERMOT—And I feel so, too. Yes, my recovery has been rapid, thanks to my nurse. (*Indicating* O'GORMAN.)

O'G.—Tut, tut, boy! It was your strong constitution that pulled you through so quickly. Harry, I wish you would add the weight of your advice to mine to induce our invalid to take a holiday. He wants to get under arms at once!

NUGENT—That would be foolish Dermot. You are not yet strong enough. Let us take a walk towards the river so as to catch the breeze. It is very warm here.

(*Exeunt* R. *in rear. Enter* SARSFIELD L *He produces a field-glass by means of which he surveys the enemys camp*)

SARSFIELD—(*Closing the glass.*)—Still no movement! As quiet as a sleeping camp! Can it be possible that the doughty William has made up his mind that Limerick is unconquerable ! I fear not. He knows too well that our defences are slight ; he will again return to the assault, for he has yet to learn that the hearts—the spirits of Irishmen, are to them sufficient substitutes for ramparts of stone and mortar. (*Turns to* R.) Ha! Who comes ?

(*Enter an* OFFICER.)

OFF.—(*Saluting.*) General, an envoy has arrived from the camp of the enemy, and he desires to see you.

SARS.—Ah, ha ! very good. I will see him here.

(*Exit* OFFICER.)

An envoy from the King ! What can be the purport of his message ? We shall see.

(*Enter* ENVOY.)

ENVOY.—Do I speak to Patrick Sarsfield ?

SARS.—Both friends and enemies know me by that name.

ENVOY—Our gracious sovereign has been pleased to make me the bearer of a message to you, which, if taken advantage of in the proper spirit, will put an immediate end to this struggle.

SARS.—An end devoutly to be wished for. Pray what is this gracious message ?

ENVOY—The illustrious William, confident in his ability to reduce this beleaguered city, yet, prompted by the goodness of his heart, is willing, nay, anxious, to save a further effusion of blood ; and, as a truly magnanimous King, offers terms of peace which you will do well to accept.

SARS.—(*Ironically*). Yes, William has already proved himself to be the very incarnation of magnanimity. Proceed.

ENVOY Knowing that your walls can no longer withstand his siege guns ; aware of a shortage of provisions in your city, and what is yet more fatal to you, a lack of ammunition, he demands the surrender of the town, and in return will allow the egress of your troops, unmolested.

SARSFIELD—Is this his message ?

ENVOY—Yes, the one our gracious king has been pleased to order me to deliver.

SARSFIELD—(*Drawing a pistol and firing it in the air.*) Then there is my answer to your king !

ENVOY—Dare you—with your crumbling walls, your dismantled fortifications—dare you to thus insult his majesty ? Must I return to the king with this insolent answer to his message of peace ?

SARSFIELD—Message of infamy ! Go ! Tell your king that in the breaches of our tottering walls he will find the glittering bayonets and stalwart bodies of Irish soldiers whose gallant hearts are their best fortifications, for they know not the word "surrender" !

ENVOY—Your message shall be delivered, but it means the destruction of Limerick, for yonder, in battle array, stands the army of England led by William, Prince of Orange !

SARSFIELD—Then tell William, Prince of Orange, that Sarsfield, Earl of Lucan, and twenty thousand Irishmen are ready to meet him, sword to sword, and bayonet to bayonet, on the walls of Limerick !

ENVOY—It shall be done.

(*Bows and exit R in rear. Enter* DERMOT, NUGENT *and* O'GORMAN, R., *in front.*)

SARS.—(*To* DERMOT.) My brave young friend, out again ! •

DERMOT—Yes, General, and eager to place myself at the head of my company.

SARS —That cannot be. Your wound is not yet well healed.

O'G.—(*Stepping forward.*) General Sarsfield, my son, though willing, is unfit—unable, to resume his command. Let me take his place. Let me fight in the ranks of Limerick's defenders, and, if need be, shed my blood for Ireland in expiation of my sin !

SARS.—O'Gorman, your prayer shall be heard. I have confidence in you and to prove it I now appoint you Captain in Colonel O'Grady's regiment ; and as soon as your son is able to resume his post I shall find another command for you.

O'G.—Thank you General ; from my heart I thank you.

SARS.—My friends, the enemy will soon recommence hostilities. I have just dismissed an envoy of the King, to whose demand for surrender I have replied in a manner befitting a commander of Irish troops. Captain Nugent please to order the buglers to sound "to arms " and you, my friends, will follow me.

(*Indicating* O'GORMAN *and* DERMOT. *Exeunt omnes,* L. *Enter* CASSIDY *and* TIM, R.).

CASS.—Tim, I'm thinkin' that the fellow from the enemy's lines got a pretty cool answer from the General, for he galloped off with a very bad lookin' face.

TIM—Yes, begorra, he looked as mad as a hatter. To the divil with him an' an' the rest of his clan ! (*A shot is heard*). What is that ! (*Both look over the wall. A second shot is heard*).

CASS.—Begorra it's the messenger that's givin' a signal to the King's throops ! Faith an' they understand it, too ! Look at them wheelin' out the cannons already ! Be the powers, Tim, we're in for it, now !

(*A bugle sounds without*).

TIM—There's the call to arms ! Come on, Micky.

(*Exeunt L. Enter R. TWO IRISH SOLDIERS who run to the guns*).

FIRST SOLDIER.—Now, Larry, we'll have another chance at the divils ! Look ! Look at the cloud of foot soldiers approachin' !

SECOND SOLDIER.—Yes, an' d'ye see the artillery over to the right ! There ! They're gettin' ready to fire ! Phew ! What a flash !

(*A loud booming, as of cannon, heard.*)

FIRST SOLDIER.—(*Looking L.*) Oh, Lord ! Look at that for an openin' in the wall ! Why the divil does'nt the Captain order us to return the compliment ? Look ! The infantry has halted, but their artillery is comin' forward. They don't think they're near enough.

SECOND SOLDIER.—What on earth's the matter with our Captain ! There's not a word out of him an' us standin' here pinin' to let fly at them !

FIRST SOLDIER.—There's the General ! What is he up to ?

SARS.—(*Outside.*) Colonel O'Grady to the front !

(*Noise of horses moving.*)

FIRST SOLDIER.—Begorra, if he is'nt orderin' up the cavalry !

SARS.—Colonel, the enemy's guns must be silenced ! Capture them !

O. G.—Men, to the capture of the guns ! Forward, for Limerick and Ireland ! Charge !

(*Music : "GARRYOWEN." THE TWO SOLDIERS look off over the wall while the music lasts*)

SECOND SOLDIER—There they go ! Now God help the red-coats ! Look Thady, who is that ridin' like mad ahead of Colonel O'Grady ? D'ye see him ? Begorra if he has'nt captured one of the enemy's cannon !

FIRST SOLDIER—Yes, yes, I see hi now ! It's Roger O'Gorman, Captain Dermot's father ! Good Lord, look at that ! Wasn't that well done !

(*Throws his hat in the air.*)

Hurrah ! They've captured ten of the enemy's guns !

(*Loud cheering outside.*)

SECOND SOLDIER—They've wheeled to one side to give us chance. See ! The enemy's infantry is makin' a charge at the breach in the wall ! Ah ! There's our captain !

A VOICE—Ready, number one battery ! Aim low—one—two—fire !

(*A flash from the two guns followed by the booming of cannon.* THE SOLDIERS *look out.*)

FIRST SOLDIER—Down they go, head over heels ! Sure they were fools to attempt it ! What's that O'Grady's regiment is doin' !

SECOND SOLDIER—Begorra they're wheeling round for another charge at the enemy !

A VOICE—Re-load, there, number one battery !

SECOND SOLDIER—Faith, that's what I like to hear !

(*They draw in the guns, re-load and run them out again.*)

FIRST SOLDIER—(*Looking out.*) There's Colonel O'Grady with his sword in the air ! They're ready for a charge ! There they go !

(*Music :* " ST. PATRICK'S DAY.")

SECOND SOLDIER—(*When the music ceases.*) By the powers, wasn't that well done ! Cut their way clean through the enemy and the cannons trailin' behind them ! There ! They've reached the gates !

(*Loud cheering outside.*)

FIRST SOLDIER—Larry, who is that over to the left—I mean the one on the white horse !

SECOND SOLDIER—Him with the shinin' helmet !

FIRST SOLDIER—Yes.

SECOND SOLDIER—Begorra if it's not King William himself, an' he's comin' forward with thousands behind him !

A VOICE—Number one battery, ready ? Fire !

(*A flash and booming of guns as before. The* SOLDIERS *re-load.*) D

(*Enter* SARSFIELD *and* O'GRADY, L.)

SARS.—(*Looking out.*) They approach in great strength led by the King himself ! We must create a diversion.

COL —You spoke a moment since of attempting to catch the enemy in the flank while we prepare the mine near the lower breach.

SARS.—I fear the risk is too great. 'Twould be next to impossible to effect the movement. I might entrust you with its accomplishment, but I cannot spare you from the walls, and poor O'Shaughnessy has been killed.

(*Enter* O'GORMAN.)

COL.—But there is another wall able to take his place—one who has already proved himself a hero!

SARS.—I know to whom you refer—Roger O'Gorman?

O'G.—(*Stepping forward.*) General Sarsfield, if you speak of a post of danger I am ready and willing to accept the command.

SARS.—But 'tis more than danger! 'Tis almost certain death to the brave fellows who will attempt it!

O'G.—I am ready to run the risk, and if man can be successful I will succeed. General, I entreat you to trust me!

SARS.—Very good. You shall have your wish. (*Looks out.*) Ha! The enemy approaches rapidly! They will attempt to take the place by storm! Well, we shall be ready. This way, O'Gorman.

(*Exeunt L.*)

FIRST SOLDIER.—Here they come, Larry! Begorra there's over ten thousand of them on this side of the river already! Ah! Our infantry are goin' to give them a dose that'll do them good!

(*Shots heard*)

A VOICE.—Steady, there, lads! Number one battery—fire!

(*Sound of cannon.*)

SECOND SOLDIER.—(*Looking out.*) How did that catch them? Begorra it hasn't stopped them at all! Faith an' I can't help admirin' their pluck—here they come on a run!

(*Reloads his gun.*)

FIRST SOLDIER.—Larry, we're goin' to have a hand-to-hand fight very soon! Some of them have already reached the walls! They're rushin' through the breaches! Oh, Lord, look at them pourin' in!

(*Sound of heavy firing.*)

Well done, boys! Well done! Larry, look at that—O'Grady's regiment is at them! Out they go, an' a good deal quicker than they came in!

(*Draws in his gun and re-loads.*)

SECOND SOLDIER.—(*Looking out.*) They're on the run! Now is our chance—we'll not wait for orders!

(*Jumps to his gun.*)

A VOICE.—Ready there, number one battery! Fire!

(*Sound of cannon.*)

FIRST SOLDIER —(*Looking out.*) Ah! They're pretty well done for! Larry, come here! Look over there! Isn't that O'Gorman at the head of a regiment gallopin' down to the river?

SECOND SOLDIER—Begorra it is! What on earth does he mean? Sure they'll be cut to pieces!

FIRST SOLDIER—They're makin' for the bridge ! Now I see what they're up to ! They want to hold the bridge to prevent any more of the enemy from crossin' ! Faith if they manage it we'll have only one half of the King's army to fight ! O Heaven, look down on them an' give them strength !

SECOND SOLDIER—There ! They've reached the bridge ! O Lord, what a fight ! Look at their swords wheelin' round their heads ! The enemy's fallin' back ! No, they recover ! Back they go again—they fly in disorder ! Hurrah ! O'Gorman has won the bridge !

(Enter SARSFIELD *and* COL. O'GRADY, *L.)*

SARS.—*(Looking through his glass).* O'Grady, they've captured the bridge ! Some of O'Gorman's men descend into the river ! They carry something which they place in a boat. What do they mean ? Ha ! What a daring exploit ! They push the boat under the bridge. Shots rain around them ! They apply a fuse—there it goes !

(A loud report as of an explosion).

SARS.—*(Closing his glass).* Well done my brave O'Gorman ! O'Grady, he has blown up the bridge—hasten to his support ! The gallant fellow must not be left unaided !

(Exeunt L.*).*

FIRST SOLDIER—*(Looking out).* Larry, I'm afraid O'Gorman an' his brave fellows'll be killed ! Thousands of the King's troops are closin' in on him ! *(Looks* L.*).* There's Colonel O'Grady at the head of his regiment !

O'GRADY—*(Outside).* Men, the gallant O'Gorman has blown up the bridge ! He is now surrounded by the enemy, but he must be saved ! Forward to the rescue ! Charge !

(Music : " GARRYOWEN.*")*

SECOND SOLDIER—There they go ! Oh, Thady, look over there to the left ! Some of the enemy are advancin' with the king himself at their head ! Now we'll have to do some fightin' !

(Both re-load their guns. Shots heard)

FIRST SOLDIER—Quick, Larry ! Let fly at them !

(Sound of cannon. They draw in their guns and proceed to re-load. Enter TWO ENGLISH SOLDIERS *over the wall. They attack the* IRISH SOLDIERS *with their swords and the latter fall back into the wings.)*

Enter CASSIDY *and* TIM L. *with rifle and bayonet.*

CASS.—*(To one of the Soldiers.)* Get back to where ye came from, ye divil !

(Attacks and drives him over the wall.)

TIM—(*To the Soldier.*) Come on ye spalpeen ! Over the wall with ye, or be the tare o' war I'll not leave a bit of ye together !

(*Forces him over.* TIM *and* CASSIDY *stand leaning over the wall while they strike right and left.*)

CASS.—Ah ha ! Ye would, would ye ! Then take that !

TIM.—Begone, ye varmint !

CASS.—Down with ye, ye ragamuffin !

TIM.—Take yer dirty paws off the wall, ye scoundrel !

CASS.—Tim, this is purty hot work ! Look ! Look ! What are they all tumblin' over each other for ? Ah, now I see—it's O'Gorman that's after them !

(*Sound of firing and clashing of weapons.*

TIM.—Hurrah ! Look at how they fly before him ! And there's Colonel O'Grady on the other side of them !

CASS.—Tim, look at Captain Dermot's father ! Sure he's as good as a whole regiment ! Doesn't he wield his sword like a giant ! Ah, but it's himself that makin' up for lost time. Begorra I can't stand it any longer—I must be mixed up in that fight ! Come on ! (*Both jump over. Enter* AN ENGLISH SOLDIER R. *He seizes the flag-pole and wrenches it from its place. Enter* DERMOT, L. *He rushes upon the soldier and they struggle for possession of the flag.* DERMOT *wins. Holding the flag in his left hand he draws his sword.*)

DERMOT—Come on hireling, and at at your peril dare to sully the flag of Ireland !

SOLDIER—(*Drawing sword.*) That flag shall be mine ! (*They fight and gradually the soldier gets the upper hand, until* DERMOT *drops on one knee.*)

SOLDIER—Surrender the flag and I will spare your life !

DERMOT—Never ! Death before dishonor ! (*The soldier renews the attack. Enter* R. O'GORMAN.)

O.'G.—Thank God, I am in time !

(*He attacks and disarms the soldier. Enter* CASSIDY *and* TIM R. *They seize the intruder.*)

O.'G.—Dermot, my boy, you are safe—the flag is unsullied, and the victory is won ! Give me that emblem of freedom that I may press it to my heart !

(*He takes the flag*)

Oh, flag of my country, I have atoned for my treason, I have redeemed my pledge, I have fought and conquered for thee ; and now in the hour of victory I promise, that wherever thy green folds are thrown to the breeze, there shall The O'Gorman be found while he has an arm and a sword to defend thee !

(A trumpet sounds. Enter SARSFIELD *and* O'GRADY, L.)

SARS.—(*Taking* O'GORMAN'S *hand in his.*) My gallant O'Gorman, let me thank you in the name of my soldiers—in the name of Ireland, for your heroic action this glorious day. The enemy has sounded a retreat ; our city is saved, and the victory is mainly due to the daunt-less courage of one of whom all Ireland shall be proud—of one who has proved himself a true soldier of his country—a hero—the hero of Limerick !

(Removes his hat).

CASS.— *Stepping forward).* General, forgive me for puttin' in a word but I can't help it ! (*Calls over the wall*). Boys give three rousin' cheers for Roger O'Gorman the father of Captain Dermot, and the hero of Limerick !

Cheering outside and

CURTAIN.

www.ingramcontent.com/pod-product-compliance
Lightning Source LLC
Chambersburg PA
CBHW030854260626
47169CB00008B/2536